AN ETERNAL QUEST FOR PEACE

AN ETERNAL QUEST FOR PEACE

A Complete Book on the Art of Living

Suvasish Mukhopadhyay

Viva Books

New Delhi | Mumbai | Chennai | Kolkata | Bengaluru | Hyderabad | Kochi | Guwahati

Publisher's note

Every possible effort has been made to ensure that the information contained in this book is accurate at the time of going to press, and the publisher and author cannot accept responsibility for any errors or omissions, however caused. No responsibility for loss or damage occasioned to any person acting, or refraining from action, as a result of the material in this publication can be accepted by the editor, the publisher or the author.

Every effort has been made to trace the owners of copyright material used in this book. The author and the publisher will be grateful for any omission brought to their notice for acknowledgement in the future editions of the book.

First Published 2011

Viva Books Private Limited

- 4737/23, Ansari Road, Daryaganj, New Delhi 110 002
  Tel. 42242200, 23258325, 23283121, Email: vivadelhi@vivagroupindia.net
- 76, Service Industries, Shirvane, Sector 1, Nerul, Navi Mumbai 400 706
  Tel. 27721273, 27721274, Email: vivamumbai@vivagroupindia.net
- Jamals Fazal Chambers, 26 Greams Road, Chennai 600 006
  Tel. 28294241, 28290304, Email: vivachennai@vivagroupindia.net
- B-103, Jindal Towers, 21/1A/3 Darga Road, Kolkata 700 017
  Tel. 22816713, Email: vivakolkata@vivagroupindia.net
- 7, GF, Sovereign Park Aptts., 56-58, K. R. Road, Basavanagudi, Bengaluru 560 004
  Tel. 26607409, Email: vivabangalore@vivagroupindia.net
- 101-102, Moghal Marc Apartments, 3-4-637 to 641, Narayanguda, Hyderabad 500 029
  Tel. 27564481, Email: vivahyderabad@vivagroupindia.net
- First Floor, Beevi Towers, SRM Road, Kaloor, Kochi 682 018
  Tel. 0484-2403055, 2403056, Email: vivakochi@vivagroupindia.net
- 232, GNB Road, Beside UCO Bank, Silpukhuri, Guwahati 781 003
  Tel. 0361-2666386, Email: vivaguwahati@vivagroupindia.net

www.vivagroupindia.com

ISBN: 978-81-309-1717-7

Published by Vinod Vasishtha for Viva Books Private Limited, 4737/23 Ansari Road, Daryaganj, New Delhi 110 002.

Printed & bound by Sanat Printers, Kundli 131 028.

X0000/H0500

I DEDICATE THIS BOOK TO MY ROLE MODEL THE SCHOLAR EXTRAORDINARY LATE SHRI NIRAD C CHAUDHURI AND MY BATCHMATE OF NIT- DURGAPUR LATE SHRI SOMENATH PAL WHO REMAINED AS AN UNBLOSSOMED BUD FOR ALL OF US.

'The day you stop searching happiness that will be the first day of your happy life.'

– *Suvasish Mukhopadhyay*

Preface

I am really glad to share my feelings and experiences about the art of living. The whole world tries to be happy but very few people are happy in today's world. People run after happiness and more they chase it, unhappier they become. However, we forget that no one can chase happiness. Happiness is the state of inner being and it comes from within. In this materialistic world people are obsessed with material possessions. The more they possess, more restless they become. Countable things can't make anybody happy.

This book is the outcome of my long cherished desire to write something about the true essence of living. I do ordinary chores like dusting, cleaning and shoe polishing. Probably for that reason I could realize the basic pleasures in these simple household works.

Since a long time I had been cherishing a desire to write a book on 'How to be happy' and after a long time I have been able to narrate my candid feelings about the art of being happy and achieving happiness in my book '*The Happiness Code*'. The feedback of my beloved readers forced me to write this book.

In my forty-seven years of life I have seen many unhappy persons, though they were quite well off. The basic reason of their unhappiness is nothing but chasing the materialistic world and feeding the false ego of post, power, authority and designation. They are not creative individuals. Even a potter is internally happy in spite of his poverty, because he gives shape to his thoughts. But the executives and managers of today's world have lost their creativity. They are always pursuing a target set by their company. The present generation is unhappy because their thoughts are ceased and their brains are mortgaged to their employers for a comfortable living.

Most of the times they forget that for the benefit of some other person their peace, health, time and freedom are ceased. Life is to be used for a creative purpose, not to be restricted for few dollars. If your mind is blocked what is the use of earning a fat pay packet? Who will enjoy it? Creative work adds colour to every tomorrow of your life and routine work makes your life very monotonous. The monotony leads to frustration and an unhappy frame of mind. You have bed but not sleep, you have gym but not health, and you have food but not appetite. What is the use of this kind of life? People purchase river-view apartments for false vanity but rarely look at the tranquil water of a river. On the contrary, a poor boatman becomes truly happy sailing his boat across a river.

I tried to reveal the truth behind the unhappiness of the people and in ninety-nine per cent cases the reasons are vague. Many of my students are in senior managerial positions in India and abroad. I am in constant touch with them. Most of them wrote candidly, they were happier when they were mere students in their college days. Opulence and happiness have an inverse relationship; though I don't want to mean that poverty brings happiness. One has to set his own limit and if a person can set his need and limitations in a proper way, he is bound to be happy. But most of the people can't set their limitations and they become the victim of unhappiness. This is the prime reason that prompted me to write this book on the art of living. In the coming years, I intend to write few more books on this subject. Each book will contain simple and heart-touching experiences of mine. I want to highlight that happiness and peace are in deep slumber within each of us. We commit a major mistake. In spite of awakening it, we search for it in the materialistic world. With each passage of effort, we distance ourselves from the true meaning of happy and peaceful life.

The melancholy and pathos of many friends and people around me lit different corners of my mind. I want this book to be the gateway through which one can get access to the corridor of happy world and they may have the glimpse of the sky of happiness. I have meticulously chosen ninety chapters and I do feel if a person goes through this book, his attitude towards life will change. I received innumerable feedback from the readers of my book entitled '*The Happiness Code*'. It gives me great pleasure to announce that lakhs of people are helped by this book and they have changed their attitude and started looking at life from a different angle. The hardest thing in this world is to influence the mind of the people. I am happy that I could do it to a great extent.

Long back I read a quotation. It stated that happiness is nothing but the bouquet made of flowers within one's own reach. How true it is! Within every unhappy person there is a hidden happy person. My mission is to awaken that happy person who is in deep slumber inside a human being. The two most important things required for being happy are simplicity and a mindset to accept the present situation. People could hardly retain their simplicity after being successful. This is the reason that people are so unhappy across the world. Keeping this in mind, I tried my best to draw the readers' mind with different examples.

No one can master over the art of living unless one understands oneself. So self-realization is essential. In today's rat race, there is no time for self-realization. All the time people are busy in satisfying the need of their clients and customers. Rarely do they take out even fifteen minutes time for themselves. As one goes high in the ladder of success, he is more and more used by the people surrounding him. In this book I have discussed very simple things in a simple way so that it can be easily comprehend and followed by readers. The first thing to be done is to stop the effort for being happy and peaceful. A flower doesn't know that it is beautiful, and only for that reason it is beautiful. You must have observed some of your friends or relatives sing when they are relaxed. If that very moment you draw their attention, they will stop singing immediately. Through this book, I tried to reach the happy inner being within a reader which is in deep slumber due to unawareness. For creating fire you don't require fire, you need a spark; similarly in most of the cases to have happiness and peace, you don't require huge wealth, what you require is to get rid of the veil of the jealousy, which encompasses you. Most of the people are misguided. They require thorough counselling and certainly their state of mind can be relaxed through proper counselling. Repeatedly throughout the book, I tried to represent the whole subject of the art of living.

At several places of this book, I have used various quotations, anecdotes and sayings of different personalities that I have recorded during different occasions. There was a time when I was a voracious reader and at a stretch I used to read twenty-two hours a day leaving even my meals and adequate hours of sleep. It was only possible, because I obtained happiness in reading. This book is the result of long tiresome hours and years of experience. Several times I failed miserably in various phases of my life. In spite of poverty, repeated failures, health problems, domestic disturbances, I consider myself as one of the happy persons of this world. Because these so-called obstacles couldn't cease my thinking process. My philosophy of positive living is not at all affected by them. Nevertheless as long as you are able to think and work freely you must consider yourself a happy person.

How to live is a great question. In my opinion, money can't buy happy life. Good living is not the exploration of the outer world, it is the digging of your inner being.

A truly happy person is untouched by the so-called success or failure of the people surrounding him. A student, who is happy, reads for pleasure not for rank and position. Self-faith is the foundation on which a happy mind rests forever.

This book is written in English for two reasons. The first reason is that English is the language which I love the most; and the second reason is, it is the only language which can reach far and wide across the globe.

This book is written for the people from all walks of life. I have taken due care so that the text can be enjoyed both by a teenager and also by an octogenarian. I am very much confident that the readers will certainly derive a great pleasure out of this book. It will certainly help them to reach the ultimate goal of happiness by observing the art of living step by step.

I have written this book on the basis of experiences of my life. I came across thousands of unhappy people, their unhappiness is very meagre. A man with a spastic child may be unhappy but if you can't afford an abroad trip then you shouldn't be unhappy. Most of the unhappiness of this world is self-created.

I have gone through unhappy experiences right from the tender age of four. In those lonely days of my bitter childhood I used to sit beside the bed of my ailing mother, who is no more. It is the experience of nearly forty-three years that has been unfurled in few pages. Several incidents are analyzed with valid and proper logic. I might not have learnt much from one single incident but whatever contents are there is the integration of the effort, analysis and logic by an ordinary person who has seen the miseries of common people from a very close angle. I am a person who doesn't feel embarrassed while carrying his own luggage, and don't depend on servant. If one just does his own work, right from polishing shoes to washing the dishes, he will find deep meaning in life.

My zeal, self-motivation, faculties of thoughts, very minute observations have helped me to write this book. This book is the outcome of my long-time research on human psychology.

I am ready to accept all sorts of comments and criticism on this book. I do hope and trust this book will also serve the same purpose like my previous book '*The Happiness Code*' on the art of achieving happiness.

I am deeply grateful to all the poets, writers, thinkers and philosophers who are quoted and referred by me in this book.

Suvasish Mukhopadhyay
professor_sm@rediffmail.com

Acknowledgements

I am thankful to my own life and its unceasing struggle. Only through this struggle, I experience the true meaning of life. My life helped me to know the meaning of happiness and the art of living. It is only due to the struggle of life with each passing day I could realize that happiness does not lie in being rich such in status, power, position and post. Happiness is simplicity, dependability, unchanged nature, modesty, caring, sharing and love.

I don't want to show any false acknowledgement to a group of people just by quoting their names. There is only one person who knows about this creation. She is my daughter Riya. I am thankful to her support, encouragement and motivation. She always wanted to see me happy in my writing venture.

I thank my family from the bottom of my heart for supporting me in this pursuit. My special thank goes to my publisher for sending my message to the mass through this book. Lastly, I am thankful to the readers of my previous books.

Suvasish Mukhopadhyay

Contents

1

Look at a Lotus

How many of us do have the time and intention to look at a lotus? We purchase park view apartment but rarely visit the parks. We purchase river view apartment but seldom look at the ripples of a river in a rainy evening. How many times you visited the terrace of your flat to look at the crescent watery moon at the rainy night? Probably the answers of all these questions will be a big 'no'. Actually in this rat race we buried the natural process of thinking and behave just like a machine. For realizing the proper meaning of life one needs to be closed to the nature. We are always confined in air-conditioned cabins and luxury cars and are miles apart from the nature. The mental condition of a person is inversely proportional to the distance from the nature. The more one becomes away from the nature, more frustration is bound to be generated. It is the rule of the nature. Just look at two people. One is from a big city like Mumbai and another is from a village. You can see the difference in the pattern of their behaviour. The man from the city will have a quick approach towards solving any problem. He will be prone to stress, tension, depression, irritation and anger. On the contrary, the man from the village may not be in a position to solve the problem but he will be stress free. It is due to the difference of the lifestyle of both of them. The person who is more close to the nature will be less affected by stress.

So for looking at a lotus you must have a relaxed mind. People say they don't get leave from their work, but if you die today, do you think your office will stop functioning? Take a break for three to four days. Reach the outskirts of your city. Stay in a small resort. Don't carry your laptop and cell phone. These are the two curses of modern civilization. If you really need to contact someone then use the phone of the resort. But you keep yourself detached from everyone, even family members. All these relationships are man made. Enjoy your aloneness in loneliness for three days. You will find different meaning in your life. Avoid heavy dinner. Get up early in the morning and welcome the rising sun through the leaves of the huddled trees. Saunter in the garden. Look at a lotus and have some conversation with it. Nature is God. It wants to communicate with you provided you are free from your preoccupations. The present generation is chained by phone calls, repeated checking of talk times, updating of the passbooks of several banks, statement of more than one credit cards, servicing of cars, some useless late night parties and lastly endless meetings. If you truly observe yourself, you will find without all these things you can survive comfortably. These are our self-created bondages. Get rid of them. Look at the water droplets on a lotus leaf. They are natural pearls. They won't wait for you for a long time. They will soon disappear as the temperature increases. Before they disappear, have a glimpse of them. Don't take photograph of it. Keep it in your mind, close your eyes and visualize it. You will be one step ahead towards the Almighty.

2

Listen to the Music of the Sphere

Once I was watching an interview of a famous personality in television. He was asked what was the key to his happiness. He replied, 'The key to my happiness is morning and evening walk in the garden of my house. I suggest everyone to go for morning and evening walk in the garden.' One can see the benefit of walking in the nature. It is beneficial to be close to the nature for sometime in the whole day, at least for half an hour.

In evening or night if you sit alone in a park or garden and look at the star-spangled sky then you will be able to discover your life in a new way. Most of us are not aware of the beauty of this life. Life is in our own hand. We may use it by chasing the false vanity of post, power and money; on the other hand we may enjoy it to its fullest extent by enjoying the nature. In night if you look at a starlit sky you will see millions of stars that are at light-years distance from you. Every star has a history. Have you imagined these things? Just lie on the grass of a garden and look at the vast dark celestial sphere dotted with stars. Look at them for fifteen minutes. Initially it will be difficult to look continuously. Gradually increase the timing from fifteen minutes to half an hour and then one hour. With each passing day your experience will change and you will find new meaning in life. It is nothing but the communication with the universe. The day you will learn how to communicate with stars, that day you will ignore these so-called materialistic gains. Common people are wasting their lives after these materialistic gains. Materialistic gain only gives stressful life and worldly tensions. Any material benefit or gain coupled with stress is considered as zero achievement.

3

Earn Blessings

Blessings are bonus in return of one's good deeds. These are GODSEND, boon that fill your life with positive vibrations. Helping needy people shower your life with humble prayers and blessings. It is hard to earn blessings of the people since vanity often comes on the way of charity. For instance, we keep all the old books, old garments for years together in the cupboards. We could donate these to needy and poor people.

Some people are very sensitive. I remember once I wanted to give some garments of my daughter to my neighbour's daughter. The garments were in very good condition. But my request touched his ego. He replied, 'Am I a beggar? Why should I take the garments already used by your daughter?' I felt sorry. I didn't have any bad intention. I just wanted the garments to be used by someone. People are of complex nature. Then I changed my mind. In the night I went to the local railway station. Many poor people were there. I distributed all the clothes among them and they were happy beyond measure. They were in real need. The half-clad children got something to cover themselves. I read the gratitude in their eyes. The blessing, which I earned, can't be described in words. In a recent survey it was proved that nearly forty per cent of the solid wastes of Mumbai city is nothing but unused foods. They are thrown by the hotels and people in the dustbin. I take regular survey of my refrigerator. In the night I go to the road with the bread and feed the street dogs. I realize their happiness. Because I know the pang of hunger. During the days of my post graduation, I had spent many afternoons in the local railway station of Uttarpara (a place near Kolkata) and used to satiate my appetite with loaf and tea in the company of beggars, lepers and stray dogs.

There is a theory called 'Action Reaction Theory' in Metaphysics. If you make anyone happy you will get double happiness and if some one becomes unhappy for you then you will get double unhappiness. So be kind to everyone and help out of your spontaneous nature whenever get opportunity.

4

Adopt Counselling, Not Anger

Whenever we see anything wrong we become angry instantly and try to solve the problem. But anger cannot solve problems. Even World Wars couldn't solve any problem though they were the outcome of angry minds. Anger leaves only carbon. Several problems can be solved by counselling instead of anger; the only thing that we require is patience. An angry mind doesn't have any logic and the persons you are angry with will hardly accept your anger. He may be frightened for a time being but your anger can't mould him internally. I would like to give one of my experiences.

I was travelling from Nagpur to Mumbai by train. Opposite to me there was a family. The couple was accompanied by their teenaged daughter. After sometime three college students came and occupied the side lower berth. Gradually they started teasing the girl. I was gradually becoming angry and the couple was not responding to them. The girl felt little uneasy. The college students were not saying anything to her directly, but indirectly she was being teased continuously. I was about to hit them. Suddenly a man from pantry came with cutlet and the father of that girl purchased six plates of cutlet and invited all those three college students and introduced her daughter to them. Further he requested his daughter to serve the cutlets to those boys. The boys became embarrassed by this kind of behaviour. They felt ashamed of their activity and within couple of minutes their behaviour had undergone total change. They were guilty from inside. In the next station they left the compartment. The father contained his anger within. So control of anger can produce such good result.

There is another example of counselling. We had a maid. One day I found her stealing some money from the pocket of my father's shirt and she was caught red-handed. I didn't take any action. I just enquired about the amount stolen by her. It was only twenty-two rupees. I advised her to keep it in the pocket again. I personally gave her twenty-two rupees and told her not to discuss this incident with anyone. She turned red out of shame. After a couple of days, I came to know that my neighbour had kept five-thousand rupees in his bedroom and left for the office. Even in his house the same maid was working. While cleaning the room she got the amount and returned it to my neighbour's wife. This is the result of counselling. One needs to cross only one barrier which comes between anger and counselling. It is the barrier of instant reaction when something goes wrong. Generally, whenever we become angry we take some decision very quickly. Most of the times those decisions are wrong. After being angry, instead of taking quick decision, if you take the decision after three hours it will be different, if the decision is taken after six hours it will be again different. So it is advisable to wait for a while and take the judicious decision. The best possible solution is to avoid anger as far as possible and replace it by counselling. In counselling we achieve permanent solution of the problem without hurting the opposite party.

5

Meditation or Sex?

Whenever we come across these two terms together we become electrocuted. There is an in-built thought in the mind of middle-class people. They think if you meditate then you need to abstain yourself from sex. It is absolutely wrong. You are born out of sex. No couple enjoys each other for producing child. Child is the ultimate outcome of their sexual pleasure. Why meditation? What is meditation? Most of us do it without knowing the proper meaning of it. Meditation is mainly done to centralize the mind and to increase the power of concentration. Most of the people are advised by the experts to go for meditation for a particular span of time and they are supposed to increase the span of meditation gradually. But most of the times they commit one mistake. They become preoccupied and they start counting times. The moment the meditating mind starts counting time it is deviated from the main purpose of meditation and the complete meaning of the meditation is lost. In life both meditation and sex are equally required. I found many people consider sex as a taboo and in spite of enjoying sex they are enveloped by a veil of hypocrisy. Why not to take it naturally? It is a natural need of human being. If it is not given an outlet it will affect the mind. Sex gives relaxation and ecstatic pleasure to tired brain and mind. You feel placid at core. Both sex and meditation give peace to heart. So both are equally required. They are just like a same number with opposite signs.

6

Happiness is a State of Your Mind

Happiness is certainly a state of your mind. Happiness comes from within. At times we are confused with preconceived notion that a rich man must be happy. Seldom it is truth. Wealth creates bondage. For being happy one needs to be relaxed. If you observe a happy person you will find him relaxed. Relaxed state of mind is the sign of happiness. Happiness is a relative term. Most of the people find happiness in achievements. For a research scholar to have the Ph.D. degree is happiness; for an infertile couple to get a child is happiness; for a shopkeeper selling of the goods brings happiness; for a sportsman winning a trophy in some national or international level competition is happiness. Thus, happiness differs from person to person. One must set his limitations. Ambition is good but fantasy is bad. Most of the people expect too much from their work. I am in the teaching profession since long time. This community is sick with the mentality of being the best teacher.

From my lifetime experience, I would state with confidence that there is happiness in sharing not in accumulating. See your happiness in others' eyes. We are proud of so many things, but have you ever thought that you can't see your own face. What a great tragedy! We are so helpless!!! Still we run after happiness. Happiness is like a grasshopper. The more you chase more it will be camouflaged. Take life easy. Accept it sincerely, not seriously. Any materialistic achievement is just like a coat on your shirt. Basically you require apparel. We should curtail our material needs as materialistic approach to life makes one extravagant and profligate.

Often we say that farmers are happy. There is reason behind their happiness. They may be poor, but they lead an honest life. They are not internally stressed. A poor man is not necessarily an unhappy man and in the similar way a rich person is not necessarily a happy one. Whenever your creativity is dead you are bound to be unhappy. Ego is the main barrier to be happy. A free, simple and down-to-earth personality will be always happy. A man who knows he is an idiot is a real intelligent man. Most of the people are under the influence of illusion. For whom you are running? The moment you are dead they will call you a body. They will not even call you by your name. When cremation takes place, seldom people wait till the end. So as long as you are in this world keep all the windows of your mind open. Let there be a flow of fresh thoughts into your mind. Only clarity in your thoughts can make you happy and try to attain clarity in your thinking process.

7

Sing Even if You Can't

It is not necessary to know the grammar of music for singing. The only thing you require is an internal urge to sing. Sing, even if you can't. Your voice may not be liked by others but you will certainly like it. Singing is a continuous flow and it can originate only in a happy state of mind. An unhappy mind can never sing. Singing soothes the inner being of a person. So make singing an integral part of your life. More you sing, more you are relaxed; and more relaxed you are, happier you become. If you can convert your life to a song that will be the ultimate achievement. For true philosophers, life is a song to get close to God and is the gateway to emancipation.

8

Self-Introspection

In Sanskrit there is an adage, '*ATMANAM JANIHI*'. It means know yourself. Self-introspection is very much required for a healthy living. Have you ever stood in front of a mirror and asked yourself who you are and where you have come from? Just do it once and you will find it very difficult to face your own image. You can face anybody for hours together but it becomes really very difficult to sustain yourself even for ten minutes. The brain stops functioning. The best way to introspect is to take the weekly review of the deeds carried out by you. Compare all the deeds and their outcome at the end of the week. We should try to do deeds which can be considered as positive and good for all.

Another way is to prepare a list of works, which are to be performed by you in the present and in the near future. Update it at the end of every month. Keep on doing works. Keep yourself engaged in positive and creative activities. Set a target. Help people. At the end of every week analyse all your deeds and access the target. Keep on trying and be regular in your attempts. Gradually, you will gain fruitful results.

Regularly give at least fifteen minutes time for meditation. Just sit in a posture in which you feel most comfortable. There is no need to sit only in '*Padmasana*' (it is a type of posture in '*Yogasana*'). If you feel most comfortable in a rocking chair, occupy that and while rocking ask yourself what are the good works done by you in the recent past. If the feedback is good you are successful and if the feedback is bad then you need to improve your performance.

9

Write Diary Regularly

One must write diary regularly. One of my friends started writing diary right from the age of nine. Not only you can keep a track record of the activities done by you, but also any time you can judge the development of your personality from it. It helps in many ways. Some of the benefits of writing diary regularly are given below.

(i) It makes you more systematic.

(ii) Automatically your daily, monthly and yearly activities are recorded.

(iii) It helps you to get some reference, which you have forgotten.

(iv) Important dates are quickly traced by the help of this habit.

In service life, importance of writing diary is very essential. You take any important personality. If you are allowed to go through their diaries, you will find many useful things. Many great books are written out of the diaries of great personalities. So imbibe this habit right from the childhood. You are never late. Better late than never. Even if you want you can start today. I know an octogenarian. He used to write diary from his school days. Now he is a widower and his children are settled abroad. He is left alone in his house in Delhi. He is mentally and physically fit. In an afternoon I visited him for discussing some English literature. I found him engrossed in a pool of old diaries and he was going through some pages of each diary. When I asked, he told me it was his marriage anniversary and seven years back his wife expired due to colon cancer. He was going through the diaries of the old years and it was a comparative study of his marriage anniversaries of different years right from his youth. He was totally enveloped by nostalgia. Have you realized why this habit is important?

10

Scan Your Past

Scanning past is very important. If you scan your past you will immediately realize where do you stand now. Let me share one personal experience with you. I know a professor who is my good friend. He was a very ordinary student in his school days and after the post graduation in Physics, he gradually improved his academic career. After his Higher Secondary, due to his bad performance in Joint Entrance Exam neither he got chance in Medical Science nor in Engineering. He was forced to take B.Sc. as his further studies. In B.Sc., he pursued his study with a half-hearted mind and his performance was not up to the mark. Then after joining post graduation, he became serious and topped in the university and after that completed his Ph.D. and post doctoral fellowship from a famous American University and now he is permanently settled in USA. Few days back one of our colleagues visited US and paid a visit to his university. He was elated to see his schoolmate. The friend who visited from India was amazed after seeing his opulence and standard of living. He had five luxury cars. When the day was over the professor called the friend to the rear side of his residence and there was a remote-controlled garage. The professor gave the remote in his friend's hand and requested him to operate it. When the garage was opened he found a very old cycle in good condition kept with due care as a vintage piece. He was little bit surprised. After asking he came to know that it was the cycle used by the professor during his school days and the cycle was the witness of all his bad days, failures and bad results. But he didn't forget it. He took special care to take it from the remote native place of India to an ultra modern campus of US based university. He didn't forget his past and that is one of the major causes of his development. So scanning past is very important. It is not possible everyday but occasional scanning of the past is important for going ahead in life.

11

Use Your Present

Most of the times either we are lost in our past or we are in the world of fantasy and future. In doing so, our costliest present slips away from our hand. We get twenty-four hours daily and the success or failure mainly depends on the efficiency of using this twenty-four hours everyday. There is a common human tendency that everybody thinks he will survive for a long time. But truly speaking nobody knows even what will happen in the next moment. He is a wise man who uses and enjoys his present to its full extent. The main thing in life is to engage yourself in creative and positive activities. Especially in the third world countries, it is observed that people become hopeless after forty and gradually there is a paralysis to their creative energy. One of my professor friends once told me, 'Two-thirds of our life is over.' I asked the logic behind this statement. After knowing the reason of this peculiar statement I was crestfallen. He answered, 'My dear, the age of retirement is fifty-eight, all of us are in the wrong side of forty. So we have completed two-third of our life.' For him, retirement is the dead end. These types of people become inactive even before three to four years of their retirement. There are examples where we witnessed people fighting World Wars at the age of eighty. Scholar like Nirad C. Chaudhuri wrote masterpiece being a nonagenarian. Actually age is a state of your mind. If you count your age by years then even at the age of thirty, you can achieve senility and if you are dynamic and energetic then even being a nonagenarian you can be creative like one of the globally famous Indian painter. It's your perspective towards life that influences it. So still there is time. If your point of view is wrong then change it right now. Use your present. It's obvious that past can't be forgotten. Past failures are like small pox scars. One of my students is an Associate Professor of Nanotechnology in a famous American University but till date he can't forget that he is a second class B.E.! But present is life and past is dead. Your past failures will be buried under the success of the present. Past will never come, tomorrow may not be there in life. But today is very much present. Use it as much as you can. Today is the foundation of tomorrow. If the foundation becomes strong the structure will be powerful and long-lasting. So don't neglect your present, don't procrastinate. Procrastination is an inbuilt vice within every human being. Procrastination is inactivity and inactivity is sin. Winter is called the season of sin, because it is the time of lethargy and inactivity. In a winter morning when the comfort and warmth of the blanket attracts you then accumulate the whole will power of the world, throw the blanket, detach yourself from the bed, leave your sweet dreams and be after the dreams of your life. Have a steaming mug of tea or coffee and go for a long walk to have a good conversation with the rising sun, which peeps through the leaves of the huddled trees.

12

Dream Your Future

Common people has only one hope and that is none other than future. People live in their tomorrows. It is always good to be hopeful. Hopeless persons are very frustrated. They count their age by years. One must not count one's life by the years. Life must be counted by the deeds and creative efforts.

I would like to share a story. Once there was a king and in his palace there was a servant. The servant had a beautiful wife and they were very happy. Once someone told the king that the servant had stolen huge amount of cash and gold from the treasury and he is planning to leave the palace with his wife. In the night the king secretly went to the servant's room and listened to the discussion of the couple. They were discussing how they will explore the world by the wealth possessed by them and how they will construct a palatial building in the outskirt of the city. The king became very angry and ordered his sentries to arrest the servant. The servant was very calm while he was brought and presented before the king. The servant laughed and said, 'Sir, what you have listened is correct. But it's not the fact. It was our imagination. I too know being a servant of yours, I can't afford a comfortable living. But what you have listened was our imagination and we the common and poor people live in our imagination only. That is the only way of happiness and comfort I could give to my beloved.' The king was astonished and spared the servant.

Dreaming future is not bad but the dream must not be a fantasy. Proper planning is required to lead a better life. Without proper planning one cannot be successful. But too much planning is also bad. Having dreams for tomorrow makes you work today for its fulfillment.

13

Don't Count Your Age by Years

I saw many people who became senile at thirties. It is unfortunate. Most of the people think thirty is the limit for creativity and after thirty, it does not continue as before. But they are wrong. There are people who are controlled by time. There is an English saying, 'If you have nothing to count then count your age.' There are some theoretical people in nature. Life is just like a Grammar book or an instruction manual for them. Their life seems to be bound with time. They have set time for everything. For instance they take their lunch sharp at 1 o' clock even if they are hungry before the time or even not.

There are people who count the number of pages before going through any book. These are the symptoms of preoccupation. If you are preoccupied you lose your degree of freedom that will block your creativity. So never behave in that way.

Now, at the age of forty-seven I still feel more active than the time when I was twenty-two. Your output is the result of your personal status, profession, liabilities, surrounding and scope. I do feel I am more free at forty-seven than I was at twenty-two. Because at the age of twenty-two, I was a student and I had to work within certain time-frame and at least for the sake of examinations, I had to follow the syllabus of the Civil Engineering curricula though I might not have liked that. At forty-seven, I feel myself as a free bird who can fly high and explore the sky. I haven't done Ph.D. and I can't go for fixed rules and it's not possible for me to do this with this free mind. Moreover, I met many knowledgeable people who don't carry high academic degrees and at the same time, saw dunces who have the doctor of philosophy (Ph.D.) but no common sense. So I lost my complete faith in degrees.

In my teaching career, I came across several guides. I personally witnessed many guides who don't even know the topic of the dissertation of their candidates. Once a professor made a beautiful comment. He said, 'If a guide doesn't misguide that is enough of guidance.' So please delete the concept of age from your mind. Never count your age by years. If you count your age by years then everything will end in tears. There was a beautiful saying, 'Forty is the youth of old age.' In my opinion, 'Forty is the youth of creative age.' So go ahead and explore the world. No one can stop you unless you stop yourself. Listen only to your inner voice. Be your own motivator. In this sad, bad and mad world, no one will come forward to motivate you. You will be your prime motivator and work hard. Practise correct things and show the world even at seventy or eighty you can be creative. In the world history we get all types of examples. Let us create one more example for enriching the history of the world. Creative mind is always young. Be young till you die. Forget the physical age. Keep the inner soul as soft as the yolk of an egg. As long as it is soft you are able to mould it and inscribe something with golden letters on it. As long as you are mentally young you will be able to accept the changes and the generation gap. The day you will not be able to accept the changes and generation gap that day you must take retirement from life.

14

Sometimes Avoid Lift

There is a saying in Bengali, it says, '*Ghora Dekhlei Khora.*' The exact English translation is not possible, but the apparent meaning is that whenever a person sees a horse, he doesn't want to walk and pretends to be lame. That means we become very much inactive whenever we get some scope to get rid of the physical labour. It's not good. Few years back lift was not in much use as we were using staircase but nowadays we hardly use staircase even for the little distance from ground floor to basement, we use lift. We would like to wait for the lift instead of the staircase available there. We are not ready to move our body. If we become so much lethargic right from the young age what will be the outcome after ten years? Whom you will make responsible if you face a severe cardiac attack at the starting of thirties? Ask yourself. Still there is time. In the keyboard of life there is no rewind button. You can only go ahead. He is an intelligent man who learns from his own mistakes but he is a wise man who learns from others' mistakes.

There is a famous soccer player. He is sixty plus and presently settled in USA. He stays at the seventeenth floor of his apartment and rarely uses lift. For keeping himself fit he always uses the staircase.

In Pune I have seen apartments in very posh localities where people only use the lift and the complete staircase is blocked and it is literally converted to garbage bin. All the wastes of the building are dumped there. Just imagine if there is an earthquake and if there is no electric supply then what will be the situation.

Modern life-style has been made mechanized and it has become the need of the hour but too much of dependency is bad.

15

What is God?

We all are familiar with the term 'God' since our childhood. It is believed that God has created this world and all the creature in this world. However, the question related to the existence of God is highly controversial. Every religion has its own concept of God. Hindu religion as it is known, has many God and Goddesses. In Christianity and Islamic faith, God is in single manifestation. Though the existence of God has always been a debatable issue but it is beyond doubt that God is a great force, which controls the nature. Just you look at a garlic and peel its layers. Can you again pack it in the same way and bring back the original shape? It is impossible. It is believed to be some supernatural power, which controls the nature. At the most that supernatural power can be termed as God. Rest of the things are imagination. People portray images or idols of God according to their own preferences and decorate them. In Hindu religion, the Goddess of wealth is named as *Laxmi* and the Goddess of knowledge is named as *Saraswati*. If any one travels within India from one state to another state he can see the change in the dress code of Goddess *Laxmi*.

In Hindu mythology *Laxmi* and *Saraswati* are two real sisters and they are the daughters of Goddess *Durga* and God *Shiva.* Though both the Goddesses of knowledge and wealth are two female forms still most women in India are illiterate and do not possess wealth. Women in rural India are the victims of superstition and male ego. There are many disturbing questions which sometimes dwindle our faith in God. Like:

(i) Why children are raped?

(ii) Why people are starved to death in African countries and in many other parts of the world?

(iii) Why there are so many religious clashes around the world?

(iv) Why corrupt politicians are leading a healthy and joyous life?

(v) Why a child becomes the victim of dreaded disease of cancer?

(vi) What is the harm caused by a child who is born with HIV^+?

There can be hundreds of questions like these, and there is no logical answer of any of these questions. In Hindu religion, they solve all the problems by the concept of rebirth. It states whatever problems one faces in this birth is due to the bad deeds of his previous birth. This is the easiest excuse, which can be given very safely. I have only one question. Why not to have the punishment of one's bad deeds in this life itself (assuming that no rebirth is there).

In Christianity and Islam, there is no concept of rebirth. If you visit any famous Hindu temples like Tirupati you will find people offering huge amount of cash and Gold to their beloved God. I don't know whether God is aware of it or not but the temple trust is very much aware of it and the total discipline of the trust can be controlled by money. By giving special fees, one may enjoy privilege there. For seeing the deity, there are separate queues and if you pay extra, your turn will come quickly. Few years back, a group of people were going to a famous temple of India and on the way in a gruesome accident all of them expired. Why God is so cruel? People were coming to see him but he didn't even allow them to survive for one more day. There is no end to this discussion, but few inferences can be drawn. God is not understood by common people, they distance themselves from the God. God is nothing but a force. Even you may get God within an inanimate object. There are many big people who have talked of God. But if you say I want to see God, they can't help. In Hindu religion, God is imagined and people worship the statues. In rural parts of Maharashtra people worship even stone just by colouring it orange and give it the status of God. However, it is devotion that matters. God exists in our faith. One cannot find him outside. He resides inside our soul in the form of truth. Truth is God and God is truth.

16

Teach Whatever You Can

The title of this chapter seems to be little funny but there is an important message behind this. Teaching gives an outlet to the stored potential of an individual. It is nothing but communication with students or anyone who wants to learn. Everyone is not supposed to be an authority of a subject. But one must share his knowledge with his juniors. It gives a special pleasure that can only be felt if you practise this habit. When I was a student of nursery, I was taught by one of my family members. Her qualification was as good as nil. She studied only up to fourth standard. But till date I remember the teaching of that lady. She tried her best to create interest in my mind for the subjects taught by her.

Often we have confusion between the qualification and the art of teaching. We have wrong notion in our mind that a teacher must be highly qualified. I do have more than twenty years of teaching experience in undergraduate and postgraduate level. From my ocean of experience, I can say with authenticity that qualification and teaching skill doesn't have any relation. Teaching means reaching the hearts of your students. It is an art. There are many Ph.Ds who are third-class teachers; on the contrary there are third class B.Sc. candidates who are great teachers. Teaching is the power of expression. If a person knows hundred per cent of a subject but if he is not able to express even twenty five per cent of it then he must not come to the teaching field. These types of persons are only fit for researches. They should only go for research. On the other hand there are persons with limited knowledge, but they are able to express it hundred per cent. These people become great teachers. One must teach regularly. It is a social service and it gives vent to your inner feelings. Just start teaching today itself and see the difference in you and your mental climate. Teaching means exchange of thoughts and sharing of information. Irrespective of your qualification, post and age you must engage yourself in teaching activity regularly at least for one hour. At least teach your own child. Nowadays people send their children to the tuition classes and don't even bother to see the progress. Only in the declaration day of the result, the parents expect good results from their children. Since they spend money for the education of the children, they think it is enough. Education is not stock market. In stock market people expect dividend after investing. In case of education one needs to be involved whole-heartedly. Unless you care for a plant, how do you expect blooming flowers out of it?

17

Gossip Occasionally

Gossiping is generally considered as a bad habit but we all at sometime do get involve in gossiping. It is looked down upon as a pastime for lazy people but often you will find that very ordinary persons giving very expert comments. Mainly during a cricket match, we find people with their personal comments regarding the playing style of the cricketers. The common people though have little knowledge about anything but discuss all sort of matters. In public transport, we see people discussing about sports, films, politics and so many other things. In fact, they are the keen observer and they are the common public. Any celebrity is nothing but the creation of the common public. Unless one is accepted by this common public he can't be a celebrity.

Therefore, gossiping is good for mind but many times, people do backbiting or criticize others while gossiping. It is sheer wastage of time. Gossiping can be fruitful if topic of discussion is healthy. Since man is a social animal and he can't be always in confinement, he needs some company to talk. Whenever we pursue a habit regularly and enjoy the freedom, we don't realize the importance of it. But the moment the freedom is curtailed, we become disturbed and morose. For instance, when fresh graduates join some service after the completion of degree; initially they become very happy for the placement, but after joining the service they face target-setting, deadlines and new challenges. They need to give the desired output and their life become restricted and stressful and they require some leisure and freedom. In today's world, software professionals are utterly frustrated. In the evening when sun kisses the western sky and the birds return to their nests then an ordinary person enjoys evening sipping a cup of tea with his family or middle class couple goes for a evening walk and do shopping. During that time the software professionals need to stay for another five to six hours before computers in their office. They get leave from the office in the mid night. At mid night the roads are deserted and the whole world goes in deep slumber. If he wants to gossip with some friend he won't be able to reach anyone. From this example it is clear that in life everything is important but at the same time excess of everything is bad. Gossiping is sometimes good for having light mood and enjoyment but at the same time one must have control over it.

18

You Can

Many times we lack motivation. Self-motivation is the power to do miracle. Once there was a man. He met with a serious accident and after that he had to undergo a surgery for the compound fracture he suffered. After the surgery, he was bed-ridden for six months and then started walking slowly by the help of crutches. He was very much traumatized and couldn't walk without the crutch. He became dependent on his pair of crutches. He decided to walk without the crutches but couldn't separate himself from it. His wife and daughter requested him several times to walk without crutch but he couldn't acquire the required mental strength to walk without it. One day one of his school mates came to see him. He was a man of strong will power. He knew how to motivate his friend. He told him, 'You are a toddler and you require your mother's finger to hold your hand for teaching you the basic steps of walking. You are a retired fellow without any strength. If you can't walk without the help of crutch then better you die. Don't be a burden on your ailing wife. How long she will support a disable husband?'

The taunt by his friend ignited the dormant confidence in that gentleman. His ego was hurt in front of his family members.

After a couple of minutes, that man slowly left his bed and by the support of the wall walked few steps and then he reached the place at the corner of the bedroom. There the pair of crutches was kept. His ego was hurt beyond limit. He felt insulted and became angry. He took the crutches and threw them through the window and came in front of his friend. After that the most unbelievable thing happened. He kicked his friend out of rage. The friend started smiling. He answered, 'I knew this would happen, because I know you since childhood. You are a suppressed volcano.' Then the friend requested the wife of that man to handover the envelope to her husband. The envelope was given to her before this episode. The envelope was sealed. The gentleman opened the envelope and took out a paper. Only two words 'YOU CAN' were written on the paper. Seeing this the man came forward and embraced his friend whose motivation helped him to get rid of the crutches for the lifetime.

19

Prefer Erosion than Corrosion

We had many extraordinary professors in our Regional Engineering College of Durgapur. I obtained my bachelor degree from there. There was a professor who was intelligent but very lazy. He hardly took any lectures. He couldn't communicate in the students' level. Basically he was frustrated. He had a brilliant academic record, but due to some personal reason he couldn't complete his Ph.D. That frustration was present throughout his life just like a spike in his boot. A great career was crushed under the grinding wheel of frustration. He was frustrated since long time. In our pre-final year, he came to teach us some Civil Engineering subject. He was erratic, short-tempered, unpunctual, whimsical and angry. All the qualities of an unbalanced personality were present in him. Practically he stopped pursuing some academic activities in spite of his talent and intelligence.

In the same department another faculty was there. He was an ever-smiling person with a very ordinary academic record. But he was very humble. He was very friendly with the students and was famous for his involvement in the entire student-related activities. He was always approachable. He completed his Ph.D.

exactly within three years before we joined the college. He was a faculty of ordinary merit but he was very hard working. Whenever he faced some doubt he used to confess it. He had the daring spirit to say, 'I don't know this. After consulting books within three days, I shall give the answer of your question.' Society needs this type of persons, who are approachable and dutiful. An intelligent person with a lazy and escapist attitude is of no use. Your intelligence won't help the society unless it is shared and utilized.

Once I approached one of the principals of a college for some work and told him, 'Sir, you please take your own time for the work. You are too busy.' He replied, 'My dear, I shall do it immediately. I can do it immediately, because I am a busy man. Mind one thing, if you want to get a work done, approach a busy man, not a lazy man.' In the rest of my life I always remembered the last line told by that Principal. Truly speaking, if you closely observe the process of erosion and corrosion you would see that both are damaging. But erosion is preferred, because it is a dynamic process.

20

Love Gardening and Farming

Have you ever pursued the hobby of gardening or farming? Just do it once and see the difference in your mind-set. I would like to share a personal experience. Once I purchased a small sapling of rose and implanted it in an earthen tub and kept it in the balcony of my house. Both my wife and me took care of the little plant. My wife nurtured the little sapling and gradually within three to four months, it became a full-bloomed rose plant. One fine morning I was enjoying a hot mug of coffee along with my favourite brand of cigarette. Suddenly I was called by my wife. She was in the balcony and a great surprise was waiting for me. When I reached the place she pointed towards the rose plant. I was surprised. I asked her, 'What happened?' She requested me to see scrupulously through the thick leaves of the plant. I found a small bud that was the result of her four months caring and nurturing. That pleasure can't be expressed in words. There are some emotions, which can only be felt, like truth, love, beauty etc.

Gradually, the bud was transformed to a full-bloomed red rose. It is just like discovering the nature. By that time the plant was dotted with innumerable buds. So this is the enjoyment one can derive out of gardening.

Farming also gives immense pleasure and satisfaction. In the cities, we don't have the scope to go for farming. But one can occasionally visit farmhouses in the outskirt of a city and enjoy his whole day with family and friends.

Once along with my colleagues and their families, I visited Ghadge farmhouse located at the outskirt of the Pune city. It was a beautiful day. Many other groups were also there for outing. One group was playing 'Antakshari' and another one was playing chess and cards. The children went for badminton and swimming. I was alone and separated myself from the rest of the crowd. I explored the nook and corner of the farmhouse. There were so many different varieties of flowers and plants. I am very close to the nature. It was a marvellous experience. Gradually the day passed by and after lunch all of us started gossiping over different topics and in the evening the whole farmhouse was gradually enveloped by darkness. The moon was visible in the southern sky and within couple of minutes all of us were below the vast canopy of the celestial sphere dotted with innumerable stars. We left the place at around 8.00 p.m. and while returning to Pune we were accompanied by the vernal zephyr, the sound of silence and whispering of the nodding eucalyptus.

21

Visit the Terrace at Night

Have you ever visited the terrace of your flat in the night? If you stay in a big city and if your apartment is a multi-storeyed building then you can have a unique opportunity. Here, I would like to share my personal experience, because personal experience enriches the matter of any book. Only through personal experience it becomes easy to reach the heart of a reader. It was the month of November 1998 and the day was *Deepavali. Deepavali* is one of the biggest festivals of India. I visited one of my collegemates in Mumbai who was staying in the 19th floor of an apartment in Juhu Tara road. I reached his place around 5.00 p.m. He was aware of my visit. He was alone as till date he is a bachelor. Presently he is the Managing Director of a multinational company which is globally famous for manufacturing good quality tyres. I was a student in the Civil Engineering Department in NIT, Durgapur and he was a student in the Chemical Engineering Department. Due to my staunch love and respect for the subject of Chemistry I had very good relation with most of the students of Chemical Engineering. After reaching his flat, I found all the arrangements for a good party waiting for me. He arranged all the things required for a good party right from my favourite brand of scotch to the brand of my cigarette. I enjoy smoking and I have a staunch fascination for liquors. Generally, while enjoying drinks up to the last drop of the last peg I don't separate myself from cigarette. Generally in one sitting continuously I consume and enjoy 5-6 large pegs accompanied by a dozen of cigarettes.

Once with one of my professor friends I had a party from evening eight to night three o'clock. I believe in the saying, 'Live life king-size.' Though I am not addicted. Many times I abstain myself from smoking and liquor for months together. I took my life as a test and I want to have the real taste of this tough test. In a country like India these habits are seen with a biased mind. There is no harm in smoking and drinking provided you don't feel guilty. Here people consume cigarette, alcohol and then they go for *pan* (betel leaf) in order to hide the smell of alcohol. This is pure hypocrisy. Either enjoy thoroughly, otherwise don't touch it.

Around 8.00 p.m., when my friend was arranging the table for a long-cherished night party, I suggested him to organize the party at the terrace for enjoying the exhibitions of firecrackers organized at different places on the occasion of Deepavali throughout the city of Mumbai. He was touched by my suggestion and both of us along with all the arrangements shifted to the terrace of that twenty-one storeyed building.

There was no one in the terrace. The beauty can't be described. The apartment was embraced by the illumination of the city from all the corners. I felt relaxed. Rarely one have this type of experience. I faced only one difficulty. Due to strong wind of the sea, it was really difficult to light the cigarette. For lighting each cigarette, I needed to hide myself behind the giant water tank located on the terrace. We had a great evening. It is one of the best evenings of my life. We consumed our favourite brands in a slow pace and it was followed by light dinner. The party started around

8.15 p.m. and we ended at 2.00 a.m. We were lost in going down the memory lanes of our collegedays. Throughout the party we witnessed the beautiful firecrackers from all the corners of the building. With each passing hour, the atmosphere became more and more cold. The illuminated billboards were another attraction from that gigantic height. There was no sound except there coming from aeroplanes which were crossing the ocean in that dead night. It was totally a different kind of feeling. I was so close to the sky.

So please have such kind of experience. Once you have it you will realize that happiness doesn't require lot of money. Happiness requires few hearts who listen to you, talk to you and really love you. It is just unfurling of your hidden wishes and sharing some good moments with someone whom you love and who cares for you.

22

Don't Plan Excessively

Planning is good but excessive planning is bad. In most of the cases, I find people plan too much. If you see people going for a trip they take too much luggage and it creates tension. One must have a right-planning.

There was a family in West Bengal. They used to stay near my house. Once they planned to visit Puri. Puri is a famous place located in the State of Orissa. It is famous for the beautiful sea and the temple of lord Jagannath. They made a great list and while going to Puri they had huge luggage. The total member in the family was four and the total number of luggage was eleven. The man was a clerk in the railway department. He decided not to spend a single penny in the train for any food. He forced his wife to take even the kerosene-stove for preparing the food. They got the cheap holiday home of railway and his wife was used more as a house help during the tour. With narrow mentality, the family went to see the beauty of the ocean. Is it possible?

Once a taxi driver was interviewed in the financial capital of India. He was asked about the kinds of passengers he came across. He answered very candidly. He said, 'Ninety-nine per cent passengers are very ordinary. They look at the meter of the taxi. Only the rest, is extraordinary. They look at the sea and forget to see the meter.' How true his observation was! This observation is the totality of his lifetime experience.

So one needs to plan less. While enjoying a holiday trip, if you need to carry your kerosene stove then better you leave the idea.

Truly speaking, these types of class three employees of railway department don't want to lose the facilities of free pass given by the Department of Railway. It is started by the Britishers. It must be stopped immediately. During those old days, there was little facility of road transport. But now after sixty three years of independence, the road transport system has been developed in India. So this type of special privilege must be stopped. The people from the postal departments don't enjoy free or subsidised communication facilities, then why these employees of Railway should be given the special treatment? Actually in most of the Government sectors we are still following the same rules framed by the Britishers. The rule, which was applicable in 1911, requires some modification or total change after hundred years. Have anyone of us thought about it?

Lastly I would like to narrate a very pathetic incidence. There was a lady in Durgapur, situated in West Bengal. Her husband was an employee of Durgapur Steel Plant. After his untimely death, the widow was survived by her only son. The son was studying in a college of Raniganj. It's a town near Durgapur. Everyday the lady used to prepare some special food for her son and after returning from the college her son used to relish those foods prepared by her mother. One day an old senior member came and advised the lady, 'Prepare any thing for your son, but don't prepare rice till he returns from the college.' It can be called an old custom or you may take it as a superstition. But the widow neglected the piece of advice given by her. After few days, in a Saturday afternoon she prepared rice for her son and till the evening the boy didn't return. Around 8.00 p.m., the dreaded news of the death of her son reached the mother. He died of a gruesome road accident. This is life. Truth is stranger than fiction. Plan, but don't have excess planning. No one knows what is in store. You don't even know what will happen in the next moment. So have judicious planning and go ahead with a moderate speed.

23

Play Some Game

Playing games are good for our over all health. Games not only keep us physically fit but also mentally and psychologically. In India, people are not much interested in outdoor games. They play indoor games like carom, chess or cards for entertainment. However, outdoor games are preferred for children in India. Earlier, sports were given adequate emphasis in schools but now computer games have taken place. Instead of giving relaxation, computer or video games increases stress level. But outdoor games give vent to the stress and makes one fit. Playing a game regularly or pursuing some sports activity regularly is important as well as helps making your day fresh and relaxed.

24

Don't Hurt Even an Ant

As far as possible don't hurt anyone even not an ant. I wake up daily at 5.30 a.m. and after having a cup of tea I immediately go to my writing table. This is my regular routine. I start my day with writing few pages and during those calm hours I enjoy some music in very low tune. I realized that for creative work, you should be alone for at least two hours per day. In the dust and din of city life it is very difficult, practically impossible to get two hours at a stretch. So at wee hours I give shape to my creative thoughts. Secondly, the efficiency of anyone becomes ten times more if he is left alone for pursuing the job undertaken by him.

One fine morning while preparing the tea I found the whole bottle of sugar is filled with a battery of red ants. It was rainy season and in the damp atmosphere the ants are more active than any other season. For a moment I was very angry and I thought to kill all of them by heating the steel container on the gas burner. But my inner conscience suggested me to stop. It told, 'Just for the sake of a cup of tea you are so impatient. They are small creatures and since the night they are storing grains for their family members. Have you not witnessed the unity of these ants? What will happen?

A few more minutes will be required to have the cup of tea! After driving them you will enjoy tea after couple of minutes.' I listened to my inner voice and gently tapped the steel container on the granite platform of the kitchen and spread one spoon sugar in the rear corner of the kitchen platform, which was partially dry. Somehow I managed to take two spoons sugar from the container, had the tea and went to my writing table. When I came after two hours, I didn't find even a single ant and all the grains spread by me at the corner of the kitchen platform were taken away by them. Just I needed to control my anger and hundreds of ants were saved.

Whenever you are at a high position, you will probably have the tendency to torture your subordinates. One can witness the competition between to torture the people who are at a lower stratum vehicles in Indian roads where big one do not allow space to the small vehicles to run swiftly. Everyone is totally preoccupied with their ego.

For the same reason in every office subordinates are unhappy with their bosses; rarely we find a boss who is appreciated by his subordinates. Just stay away from the ego and show respect to your juniors. Don't hurt anyone unnecessary. You need not remind your subordinate that he is junior to you. He knows it very well. In this world, everyone is aware of his position and your position. There need not be an exhibition of ego. That is damaging and corroding for the human relation. Human relation is the foundation on which the whole society is standing. If that foundation is disturbed then the relation between the people will be affected and once the relations are strained no good thing is possible. Human relation can be compared with the nucleus of a living cell. If there is damage to the cell wall, it can be recovered within some time, but if the nucleus is affected then there is no remedy. For this reason cancer is so dangerous. The nucleus of the cell gets affected in cancer. So take care of everybody in and around you. Love begets love, hatred begets hatred and respect begets respect. Life is just like an echo. Do good things, behave in a proper way. Certainly you will enjoy the proper feedback from others.

25

You Lost Your Spectacle, other Lost their Vision

We are extremely selfish and materialistic people. Once my uncle decided to clean his apartment in his residence. He was staying in Nagpur since 1948. It was the year of 1995. Before the festival of Deepavali, he took the cleaning drive. He didn't have any child. My uncle and aunt brought up the daughter of my aunt's brother. Both my uncle and aunt were extremely materialistic and my aunt was one step ahead of my uncle. I was also present there on that day. After the breakfast, we started the cleaning drive before they are disposed off. It was a hectic work and it was not at all possible to clean the whole apartment in one day. In the first day, we mainly cleaned the bedrooms of the apartment.

There was a huge garbage and many wastes. We stored them in one corner of the balcony to dispose them. After the lunch all of us slept, because we were quite tired. Only my aunt didn't sleep. She continued to watch television. Around 5.00 p.m. we got up. My uncle prepared tea and awakened me. He said, 'Please come with me to see the eighth wonder of the world.' I couldn't get him. I followed him. He brought me to the corner of the balcony where we stored all the useless garbage before the lunch. I found more than eighty per cent of the things were missing. It was the act of my aunt. When we went to sleep, she gave us the false excuse of watching television. Once we slept; she picked up most of the things from the wastes and again placed them in their previous positions. For her even a ten-year-old showpiece was important. Then my uncle asked her why she did that. She didn't have any satisfactory explanation. But from her body language one thing was clear. She didn't want any of us to disturb her. She was excessive materialistic. She spent her whole life after useless things like utensils and house hold knick-knacks. These people do not know the term charity, sharing and caring.

After few days without informing us my aunt went to a temple. After returning from the temple she didn't find her spectacle. She started howling and accused my uncle, as if he had lost it. It was the gruelling summer afternoon of Nagpur. The temperature was around forty-five degree Celsius; she forced my uncle to go to the temple to search the spectacle. I couldn't leave him alone. I too accompanied him. After visiting the temple, we met the head priest. He intimated that the spectacle was found. It was kept in the office of the temple. We took it back, thanked him and returned to the house. My uncle told me not to disclose the fact. After returning, he straightaway denied everything. He exclaimed, 'I knew very well we won't get it in the temple. Unnecessary we were heckled by you.' My aunt was visibly disturbed.

In the evening, my uncle took his car and requested all of us to accompany him. We didn't know our destination. Within half an hour, we reached the outskirt of the city and my uncle entered the gate of an old building. It was a blind school. Some blind boys were sitting in the staircases.

Then my uncle got down from the car and requested all of us to accompany him. We stayed at a distance and then my uncle told my aunt, 'My dear, look at this teenaged boys and girls. At this age they are blind. Most of them are blind by birth. You were howling since morning for a meagre spectacle. It can be purchased just by two hundred rupees. You have sight but lost the vision. Here is your spectacle in my pocket. Just take it and in future don't lose it and blame others. You left it in the temple itself. I brought you here just to show you the condition of these handicapped children.'

My aunt was speechless but till date it's not clear to me how much my uncle could convince her that evening. As long as we are physically fit, we care for very minute things, because we don't realize the gifts of God.

26

A Positive-Minded Cancer Patient

One of my very close family members was attacked by lung cancer. That time his age was sixty-seven. He was a chain smoker but he was happily pursuing retired life without any liabilities. Suddenly he had a severe cough problem but there were no symptoms of any type of cold. Initially he ignored it but the severity of the cough didn't subside. He consulted his house physician, but he couldn't find anything wrong with him. He returned happily. Then within few days, he started losing weight and he started feeling very weak even after the slightest amount of physical work. Again he reported to his house physician. This time also the physician didn't find anything wrong, but had some doubt. He recommended him to a chest specialist. The specialist recommended Biopsy and routine blood test. Generally people get very nervous by the name of Biopsy. The person was very firm. He didn't say anything to anyone. Always he wanted to see everyone happy. The Biopsy was done.

After a couple of days, he found his daughter sobbing at one corner of her bedroom. When inquired he was shocked. He kept the cash receipt of the Biopsy test in the pocket of his shirt. While washing the shirt his daughter got it. Till that day the report was to be given. His daughter forced him to accompany him to the hospital. The gentleman couldn't prevent her from coming with him. When they reported the hospital the report was ready. The doctor handed it over to him. He was detected fourth stage lung cancer and the doctor was very rude. He told, 'Your days are numbered now.' The man replied, 'Dear doctor, no one can say when someone will die. My sixth sense says your days are numbered too.' Literally it happened. After three weeks the doctor died of a gruesome road accident but the said cancer patient survived for another four and half years.

After he was detected cancer, he made a statement. It is still etched in my mind. He stated, 'I am sixty-seven. I enjoyed enough in my life and till the last day of my life I will keep on smiling. I shall not let others know that I am a cancer patient. Either today or tomorrow I shall have to die. Let's have a joyous death. Thank God, ultimately I got the punishment for my smoking habit. There are small children who are the victims of this dreaded disease. Let God take my life in spite of those innocent kids.'

The dreaded disease didn't take life from him. For Chemotherapy, he was admitted in a reputed hospital of Pune. When I went to see him, he personally accompanied me to the nearby hotel for a good dinner. Hotel foods were totally restricted for him. His diet chart was totally fixed by the dietician. It was very simple and a common man can't take that. After scrupulously going through the menu card he placed the order. I was accompanied by one of my friends. Still the needle of the saline was attached to the rear side of his palm. The people of the whole hotel were observing the bold attitude of that old gentleman. He had chosen the menu in such a way as if he was ordering for satiating his own appetite. After three cycles of Chemotherapy he had a slight relief. For all the sittings of Chemotherapy, he had to come to Pune. Everytime I used to meet him.

Then after few months, again the problem intensified and he was operated. I was personally present during his operation. During those days, I was posted in Govt. College of Engineering, Karad. I had taken half pay leave for his operation and throughout the span of his operation I was present in the hospital. After operation there was stream of visitors to see him. The old gentleman was a trade union leader. Even at that condition, he took care of every visitor. He was very much aware of the food habits and taste of all his well wishers and visitors. He used to keep chocolates below his pillow. He used to offer chocolates to each of the child visitor accompanied by their guardians.

Cancer couldn't make him weak. After Chemotherapy, he lost all the hair. Out of sheer love, his office colleagues used to address him as DADA. Once one of his colleagues commented, 'Dada lost all the hair, for that I bought this Gandhi cap for Dada.' He humorously replied, 'Cap is not required. Baldness is not harmful as long it is external. At this age I require a balanced head, not hair.' Even at the deathbed he was so humorous.

Lastly he was sent for radiotherapy. It was a course of forty-five days. He had nobody in Pune except me. He stayed with me. He was so jovial that he changed the total atmosphere of my house. Initially for one or two days, I accompanied him for the radiation. Then he told me not to accompany him and not to remind him that he is a cancer patient. He told me not to disclose his disease to any of the members of my society. He stated, 'Enquiry of the people is more irritating than cancer. If they ask you say I came for a vacation.' But people in India are excessively curious and within few days the members of my society and my neighbours came to know the purpose of his visit. Once in the market a curious Bengali gentleman asked him, 'How the radiation is going on?' He commented smilingly, 'It's fine, not hazardous for the society.' Though he was angry for this unwanted curiosity still he maintained the balance in his temper and humour in his behaviour. Even in radiation centre all the staffs and doctors were surprised by his will power. He stayed in my house for one and half months. My wife was very happy with him. She gained five-kilo weight during that span in spite of her huge workload.

One day after coming from office, I found that he repaired all the broken hatch bolts of the doors and windows of the quarters and cleaned all the glass panes of the windows. In the evening he used to accompany us to the nearby market and literally he used to cook variety of dishes both vegetarian and non-vegetarian every day. During his stay all of us enjoyed the company of a cancer patient for a span of one and a half months. After the tenure of radiation therapy, he returned to his place. His last visit was in June 1999. Again he stayed with us for five weeks and departed for his place after the treatment. After the detection of cancer he had to leave smoking but he couldn't separate himself from his love for cigarette. He was obsessed with his smoking habit, which he pursued nearly for forty-five years. In a lonely afternoon, I saw him staring at some empty packet of cigarettes and lost in thoughts. I used to take empty packets of cigarettes for him from the nearby cigarette shop.

In 26th December 2003, I received a phone call from his daughter and came to know that he left us forever. I was too sad. Still he is my inspiration. He was the man who influenced me and motivated my spirit. He taught me how to talk. He was a person of command and I learnt the literal meaning of command from him and applied in my teaching career and day-to-day life. He was a great leader. Till date all his family members and colleagues remember him with love and respect.

27

Play Some Instrument

Music has a great impact on human being; even animals are influenced by music. It can be either in the form of song or in the form of some musical instrument. All people can't sing, because it is a God gifted quality. But no one can resist you from learning some instrument. It is considered as a positive engagement. Many people don't get the desired scope in their childhood or boyhood. But if you want to learn something then don't allow your age to play the role of a barrier. I know a person who didn't even have an iota of knowledge about any musical instrument or music. He decided to learn piano at the age of fifty-seven. Today his age is seventy-eight and he is a top class Pianist. It is just his hobby but this hobby helps him to engage himself at this old age. There is a saying in English, 'Senility itself is a disease.' But if a person becomes creative and keeps himself engaged in creative activities then he will be evergreen and he won't allow his senility to mar the core of happiness. Learning any musical instrument, gives positive engagement in old age when one doesn't have enough work.

28

Have a Big Picture in Mind

Have a big picture in mind means have a big aim. There are some people who always say, 'I am a small person'. These types of people are highly negative at core and are very cynical. They are just like a submissive quadruped in front of his master. Sycophants flatter their boss and irritate their subordinates. These people lost interest in their life and they have nothing to do except the routine work. They criticize others, they lack vision, they can't stand others enjoyment and success. They are dissatisfied with what they have but don't try for further progress. They are hypocrites and they say that their ambitions are very limited.

Unless I share some of my experience it will not be completed in its interpretation. There was a lower division clerk in a Government office. He was a good student and his specialization in graduation was History. He was suffering from serious inferiority complexe and lost all the hope for the future. He was only twenty-three years old. He was brilliant, but he had a cynical attitude. One day the director of the office called him. The director was a senior officer of UPSC cadre. He came to know about this clerk. He asked him straightaway, 'Do you want to continue as a clerk or want to do something else?' The man replied, 'Sir, after two years I will be able to appear for the departmental examination for the rank of an upper division clerk. So I don't require any preparation now. I shall start before six months of the exam.' The director was surprised at his reply. He said, 'Mr Chatterjee, you have sight but you lost your vision. You do possess only the bookish knowledge. If you are asked what is life you would say, 'In the syllabus or curricula of my graduation there was no chapter on life.' Basically you people are like earthworms. Be dynamic man. Still there is time. You are only twenty-three, I am fifty-six. Why don't you prepare for IAS examination? I shall sanction special leave for you.'

After meeting the director, Mr Chatterjee was disturbed. This type of lazy people feels disturbed if they are motivated or if someone talks in a positive way. These people want to lead a very lazy life but they are jack-of-all-trades. They never play any game, but give comments on how to play the game. They never take part in any social activities, but they are the staunch critics of the society, they never cast votes, but criticize the political scenario of the country.

After the advice of the director Mr Chatterjee was actually not happy. Because he was quite happy with the position of a lower division clerk. He was a person with low self esteem.There are some people who prefer to remain in darkness. Mr Chatterjee belonged to that category.

After few days the director was transferred and there was a farewell party arranged for him. In the last day the director was searching Mr Chatterjee among the staffs but came to know that Mr Chatterjee was in casual leave. The truth was that Mr Chatterjee wanted to avoid director in the public. So, he took one-day leave. Till date Mr Chatterjee is remained as an office super (equivalent to a senior most head clerk) in a Govt. sector of West Bengal. Neither he tried for IAS nor did he appear. The advice of the director didn't have any impact on him. He is very famous in the whole office for his erratic and cynical attitude. He remained unmarried. No girl was there who could readily accept him. This is life. Just due to the negative mindset a capable man remained in darkness forever. Brilliancy coupled with negative mindset is a dangerous thing. It produces only negative output. It is much easy to walk with an idiot than with a brilliant but negative-minded person.

29

Have Some Role Model

It is important to have a role model as an inspiration. In my life, I consider the great author and thinker Late Nirad C Chaudhuri as my role model. In every sphere of life, people must have a role model. To have a role model doesn't mean you should copy him or her, but the role model becomes the source of constant inspiration. In student life every student wants to have a role model. In every school or college there are few teachers or professors who become the role model of the students. Nirad C Chaudhuri is my role model for my writing career. Because I had to struggle a lot to be a writer and there can be a thousand page book on how I got series of rejections before my first book *MY STUDENTS OF FAR AND NEAR* was published.

But let me share an exclusive experience of mine. Till date my undergraduate teacher Prof D.P. Mazumdar is my role model as far as teaching skills are considered. Professionally I am a teacher. Whether a person is a professor or a primary school teacher ultimately he is a teacher. Prof D.P. Mazumdar and his teaching techniques inspired me a lot and he is the only person in the world whose teaching techniques inspired me tremendously to be a teacher in my later life. I had decided to be a teacher since I was a college student. I was not a topper; more precisely speaking, I didn't want to be a topper. Toppers run after marks and if anyone runs after marks he becomes deviated from the actual subject knowledge. Teaching is a relatively low-paid profession in our country. In spite of knowing that I accepted it gladly. Not only I accepted it but also I refused many other lucrative offers in my life. They were lucrative only from the viewpoint of money. But money earning was not my only motive. The influence of mind over mind is the greatest influence of the world and same thing happened during my college days. Prof D.P. Mazumdar taught us Applied Mechanics, Strength of Material, Fluid Mechanics, Advanced Fluid Mechanics and Hydraulic Machines. He was a versatile genius; I never saw any note or book with him while delivering any lecture. He can be called a moving lexicon of Engineering and Technology. Even he used to forget the name of the subjects. Because at a time he used to tackle three to four subjects for undergraduate and postgraduate level. We were amazed by his teaching skill. Still he is very much active in his Kolkata-based residence after retirement. The teaching skill and strategy of this great master influenced me to accept teaching as a mission in my later life. So to have a role model is very important. I do agree that now it has really become difficult to have a person as role model. Because most of the people are chasing the materialistic world. If you don't get a suitable person as a role model then search some character in history. There are many stalwarts who are no more. But they can be taken as a role model of your life.

30

Love the Animals

'Animals are more loyal than man.' It may be a controversial statement. I want to be non-committal regarding this. But certainly animals are loyal, because they are innocent and their thinking process is not like ours. In the animal world, everything is instant. There is no concept of bank or refrigerator in the animal world. They too store, but very little. You must have seen ants to store grains during dry season for the emergency period, but there is a certain limit to it.

From the dawn of civilization people have been very cruel towards animals. Animals are used as foods. Hunting is not only for the sake of food but also for pleasure. Many species are rare and many are extinct like blue whale. Our need is too much and for most of us they are taken for recreation. Once in a zoo, people offered fruits to monkeys and within the fruits they embedded metallic pins. It is the ultimate cruelty. Why this sadist approach with the innocent animals?

In our locality there were many stray dogs. Once one family allured those dogs by pieces of breads and when they came for eating they were chained and beaten mercilessly. Is it civilization?

If you want to hit somebody hit from the front side. Don't attack by wearing a veil of hypocrisy. It is even worser than the act of a diplomat. Animals require lot of care and love. In a country like India, the population is so huge, it crossed even one billion long back. People are starving in this nation, how you will feed the animals? Someone was telling that India's population is one-sixth of the global population and just by coincidence India also possesses the highest population of the cattle of the world. The readers are requested to read between the lines and draw the inference that suits their mind.

The peculiarity is that the cattles are innocent and the cost of cattle is much more as compared to the useless population of the country. There is a group who just pollute the country; another group is giving birth to terrorism. So cattles are more preferred than these types of citizens. Celebrities are arrested for hunting extinct species and they are released in bail. The political power and ill-gotten money are used to justify the misdeeds of big shots. In the name of democracy, we balance all the equations. In this country, democracy is used as a tool for being relieved from the jail for the misdeeds done by the wicked people.

Even there are huge grants for the zoological gardens located in different pockets of the country but there are semi-starved animals. Where the fund is flowing that needs to be traced and vindicated. Doctors don't have love for their patients. Teachers don't have love for their students and in-charges of the zoological gardens don't have any feelings for the inmates of the zoo. If this becomes the result, failure and mismanagement are inevitable.

Still there is time. Counselling can create good result. Throughout the country there should be counselling centres through which we will be able to guide the common folk. Gradually result will be there and the gulf between the animal world and human being will reduce. Like each one teach one. If every family keeps a pet and take care of it that too will create a great revolution.

31

Power of a Candle

Probably very few of us are aware of the power of a candle. Once I was gossiping with one friend in his posh apartment of South Kolkata. The interior decoration of his house was beyond description. Only the lighting and decoration of the drawing room was worth lakhs of rupees. In the evening, we were sharing some light moments over a cup of coffee. After nearly half an hour, another friend joined us. He was slightly different person than others. He was not abnormal, but at the same time he was little different. His thinking pattern was totally different from all other normal human beings. Suddenly he lit a candle. We were irritated by his prank. In that illuminated drawing room, the candle seemed to be an odd man out. We didn't care for it and practically ignored it. Then he went ahead and switched off the main switch below the staircase. The whole drawing room was having only one source of light and that was nothing but that candle. Then each of us realized the value of the light produced by the candle. Whether it is a halogen lamp or candle, the basic purpose is same. The basic purpose is to get rid of darkness. What can be more powerful than light? Whether it is light of the sun or light produced out of a candle. Most of us know that light is energy but most of the times we forget that light can't be seen. Whenever light reflects from the surface of an object we see the object. So noone should ignore the power of a candle, because it also produces light and removes darkness.

32

Empathy, Not Sympathy

Once there was an argument between two stalwarts. The subject of argument was very typical. The subject was whether concentration is more important or attention is more important. Ultimately both of them came to the conclusion that attention is more important than concentration. Because to concentrate in some matter, we whip our minds and make it concentrate in one point. It is really difficult for anybody to concentrate in some matter for more time and it is artificial. Why to whip the mind? It is recommended to attain that state of mind which doesn't require any external force.

In the same way it is stated that empathy is more important than sympathy. There are people who don't like sympathy. Whenever anybody shows some sympathy to us we feel belittled. Sympathy is nothing but one kind of pity. On the contrary, empathy is much more important than sympathy. The dictionary meaning of empathy is 'Power of identifying oneself mentally with person or object of contemplation.' We need to go deep and understand the core meaning of empathy. By showing sympathy to a person we make him small in his eyes, but by showing empathy to a person we honour him. So it is always advisable to have empathy for others rather than sympathy.

33

Read for Pleasure

Most of the times we read for some purpose. Sometimes for examination or for other reason, but not for pleasure. Have you ever read for pleasure? Just do it once and see the result. It's amazing. If you read with a purpose in mind, you miss the basic meaning of life. If your reading is proper you will automatically know your subject and certainly you will fare good in the exam. We do the opposite thing. We first see the exam date and become preoccupied. The moment a mind becomes preoccupied, it loses its creativity and the flexibility. The thinking process gets restricted. The whole system becomes stressful and mind loses its actual efficiency. Your mind should be like a thermocoal in sea water. Let it float properly. So always read for pleasure. Even subjects like Physics, Chemistry and Mathematics should be read for pleasure. In one incident in my childhood I had to go through the fourth chapter of my Chemistry book. Before reading, I was counting the total numbers of pages of the chapter. Suddenly my elder brother noticed it. He was very good in Chemistry and famous for his voracious reading habit. Both of us had the capability to read at a stretch for twenty-two hours. He immediately suggested me,

'Don't count the pages. It seems to be you are setting a target. Don't do that. Start reading, when you feel tired take rest for a while and start again. Convert the subject of Chemistry to a storybook.' What a golden piece of advice I had from him that day! After that particular incident, throughout my life I obeyed this advice and that helped me enjoy reading. You too adopt the same thing. You do it at least once and taste the enjoyment in reading. You will certainly get different flavour in reading. It will be just like browsing your favourite website. The more relaxed the mind is the more is the grasping power. The mind shouldn't be locked. Your mind should be porous, so that information and knowledge can percolate. Only unconditional reading can give this state of mind.

34

Failure is a Relative Term

What is Failure? Failure is nothing but failing to reach the desired target set by anyone. There are two types of failures. One is called absolute failure and the second one is relative failure. Suppose a couple wants child but they are unable to have it. Let us assume that after scrutiny, it is known that one of them is infertile. So this is a case of failure. On the other hand, another couple wants male child, but repeatedly for four times, they gave birth to four daughters. This is also failure but certainly not absolute failure. In this case they are unable to set the target fixed by them. Obviously, the first target was to have a child; once the first target is fulfilled the second one came to the picture. But if you seriously think and look at both these cases you will find nothing is failure. In life, ups and downs are inevitable. A person is not expected to explore all the avenues of life. So one has to accept it and one needs to find a golden mean. The best way for an infertile couple is to adopt a child. For every problem, there is a solution. It's up to you, whether you want it or not.

Generally, the human mind is unhappy. I saw one of my students crying even after securing ninety-nine out of hundred in a subject.

He was not happy for the ninety-nine marks but the one mark not secured by him was sufficient enough to make him unhappy. We are more prone to unhappiness and we define our failures in our own style. Failure is a relative term. For someone not to have child is a failure, for another person not getting promotion is a failure, for a nubile lady not getting married in time is a failure, for a mountaineer, inability to capture a peak is considered as failure, for a jail inmate confinement within four walls is a failure, for a school student a bad marksheet is a failure. So there are hundreds and thousands of ways to express it. But if one becomes morose with them then he can't go ahead. Life can be compared to a journey. These failures are thorns spread on the road. They will prick our feet. We have to detach them and go ahead. If we sit and start thinking the cause of pricking then we will not be able to complete the journey. Don't take any failure seriously, because it can't be changed. Only vindicate the reason of it. If it is your mistake then don't allow the mistake to repeat for the second time. Success and failure are inevitable parts of everyone's life. One should remember that.

35

What should You do Now?

It's a million dollar question. What should you do now? I don't know your age. Your age may be twenty or it may be even eighty. So whatever your age may be it is immaterial. You need to have a positive frame of mind for the rest of your life. You need to scan your past and make a list of mistakes committed by you. You are not supposed to repeat those mistakes for the second time. Secondly, you are supposed to ask yourself what you really wanted to be. In this world, more than ninety per cent people wanted to be something else. They say due to luck they are misplaced. But I would say due to greed, wrong counselling, wrong notion and wrong decision they are misplaced. There are people who wanted to pursue their career in music but they became bankers, someone wanted to be an artist but became a doctor. If one is deviated from his choicest field of study that becomes the most unfortunate thing in life. In my life I didn't allow it. As a result I had to accept less lucrative teaching job, where monetory benefit is practically nil. But as far as job satisfaction is considered, I state with authenticity and guarantee that I am very happy with my students and the teaching-learning process. So if you are deviated from your choicest field and if it is too late to go back to that field then at least give one hour per day for that field. Let us take the example of a doctor who actually wanted to be an artist. In addition to his medical profession he should start giving at least one hour for painting. That will help him. He will have internal peace. It will soothe his inner mind and soul from the core.

You must go ahead with indomitable spirit. Try to live the rest of your life with a good spirit. Love people, love the surrounding and love the nature. Love is the greatest force in the world. It can transform everything. Even the criminal bends in front of love. It is nothing but the influence of mind over mind and that is the greatest influence. Don't run after any award, honour or certificate. Those are the outcome of your creation. How many awards will you display? Who will see them? Try to engrave your name in the heart of the people by your good deeds and benevolent nature.

36

Why the Flame Always Goes Up?

You must have seen the flame of a lamp or candle. No force in this world can bring down this flame. Nothing is more pure than fire in this world. Fire is strength, fire is power, fire is compared with an honest soul. An honest heart never bends. I can give my own example. I am not boasting of myself but I am telling you the candid truth. In my college days, I found many of my friends copying in the examination. I couldn't prevent them from copying; at the same time I didn't try to prevent them from adopting wrong means for passing the examination. Why they would listen to the philosophy of their classmate? Most of them are in very big posts and positions but their college days are very much known to me. It is very difficult for most of them to face me. It is totally impossible for them to say that whatever I am writing is wrong.

Once in an examination, I was completely flustered and I was unable to answer the question. My friend sitting beside me was copying and he realized my problem. For him, it was a golden opportunity to trap me. Because none of them liked my honest and straightforward nature. These types of persons want to have at least one black record of every individual in their pocket.

If someone knows one of your weak points, it becomes really difficult for you to behave in a straightforward manner with that person. Either they blackmail you or they ignore you. My friend also wanted the same. His basic motto was to break my honest background. But I too was very rigid and I didn't bend to it. At the end of the examination he said, 'Please have some help, otherwise you will fail.' I said, 'I prefer to fail rather than take the help from you.' In that examination I didn't fail but secured very less marks. All of them secured more than me.

But due to my sincerity towards the subjects, I remember most of the portion of that subject, what I prepared in those days but my batch mates are miles apart from the subject. For them exam is a game just for passing, but for me examination is not important but the subject is important. The subject must be respected. This is the reason that I couldn't earn money like them. But I remember all the subjects I read in my student life. Even after thirty years of my Higher Secondary examination, I can chant the whole Periodic Table of Chemistry very easily. It is only possible due to the internal urge of mine and my love for education. It is possible because the flame always goes up.

37

Motivate the Mass

To motivate the mass is a very difficult task. It is even difficult to motivate a single human being. Let me share an experience of my life and from that it will be clear how to motivate the mass. Generally whenever anything is personal we take very much care of it; but the moment it becomes public we ignore it. As an example we always take care of our own books but we don't care for books kept in the library. This is the inbuilt attitude. Unless the guardians and parents are serious about the matter, it won't change.

Let me come to the point, what I was going to discuss. In Pune there was a library in an institute. There were at least a dozen of staffs to take care of the library. The main threat was theft of books by the students and tearing out of pages from the books. One day, the Principal called all the students. In spite of scolding them, he took a very beautiful meeting. Through the meeting he motivated the students. Motivating the students mean motivating the mass. The briefing of the meeting between the Principal and students are given below.

Principal: 'Good Morning boys.'

Students: 'Good Morning sir.'

Principal: 'Do you know what for you are called today?'

Students: 'Yes sir, it is regarding the library.'

Principal: 'All of you are aware that in spite of one dozen staffs in the library books are being stolen from the library. Except you people, no one uses the library. So none else than you are responsible. I won't scold you. But if this mischief continues, what will be the condition of the library after five years. The student who will join this college after four to five years, what impression they will carry about their seniors and alumni of this college. Have you ever felt it?'

After the statement of the Principal, most of the students felt sorry because the Principal reached their hearts by his soft counselling. One boy was very innocent. Suddenly he stood up and answered, 'Sir if you don't punish me then I shall tell the truth.'

The Principal assured him that no punishment would be there.

The boy replied, 'Sir, I am touched by your words. Till date I have stolen nine books from this library. Tomorrow I shall return all of them. Apart from that I know many others who damaged the books and removed the pages from the books. I know many boys who possess many other books and most of them are stolen from this library.'

The Principal gave them the opportunity to surrender and within seven days over two hundred books were returned. After that the Principal called each of them and talked to them and congratulated them for changing their behaviour. He was able to reach their mind. If you want to control a thief, you need to keep all your belongings with him. At least trust him once.

After that the Principal shifted nearly fifty per cent library staffs to other departments. Because most of them were worthless and they used to work half-heartedly. They knew everything but never tried to control this theft. For them it was a duty. Their attitude was, 'Why to bother. It is not my personal book.'

The Principal was very intelligent. He studied the behaviour of the staffs and students and started giving more responsibilities to the students; the library timing was also changed. Initially it was 10.30 a.m. to 5.30 p.m. Now it is 8.00 a.m. to 8.00 p.m. In the extra hours, one staff is deputed but most of the works and management are shared by students' representatives. The students started feeling as if it is their own library, not the institutional library. They became possessive about their library. They were proud of their achievements. The cases of theft reduced gradually and after five years the number of theft case was zero. The Principal was transferred before two years but the trend set by him is continuing till date. After his retirement while leaving the college he donated his personal collection to the institutional library. Even the senior students donated books in regular basis to improve the library and today it is one of the best institutional libraries of Pune. Do you get the meaning of 'Motivating the mass?'

38

Maintain Self-Respect

If anybody asks me what is the costliest thing in human life then I would say nothing is costlier than self-respect. It is up to a person. Self-respect is very closely associated with sensitive people. Generally there are some factors on which the degree of self-respect depends. Even a very poor person may have self-respect on the contrary a very rich person may not have self-respect. There was a saying of a famous philosopher: If a child is kept with a master for seven years continuously then that seven years time is more than sufficient to mould the child. The teaching of the master has a lusting impression on the child's mind. Seldom can he come out of it. For coming out of it, he requires reverse counselling which will undo his previous learning. We are not going to discuss about the quality or ability of the teaching of the master. But certainly each child is directly or indirectly influenced by his or her master. For a child the master becomes the role model.

In a hostel there were some students. There was great difference. One of them was very rich and another boy was very poor. One day the poor boy required some money. Other students suggested him to take it from the rich boy. The rich boy was very open-minded and he was close to the heart of the poor boy. But the poor boy did a different thing. In spite of laying his hand to his friend, he started doing part time job in a Civil Engineering site. By this way, he fulfilled the requirement for money. This is called self-respect. People will want to give you, but preferably avoid it. Once you take it they will be happy. If you want for the second and third time they will be annoyed, and if you keep on wanting things from people they will hate you and they will start maintaining distance from you. So retain your self-respect and be a man of principles.

39

Don't Close Your Books

Most of us read for passing examinations and getting a job. Is it the purpose of study? Are you waiting for death or to enjoy life? Everyone knows man is mortal. Don't adopt a dull lifestyle. To pass an examination and to get a job is the routine procedure. If you study very seriously then you will certainly get the job but if you study in a relaxed way then also you will get the job. It is not the question of getting jobs or passing examinations. It is the question of your perspective towards your life.

In our days of schools and colleges, we used to study regularly for three to four hours. Most of us close our books permanently after getting the job. Have you ever thought of pursuing your studies as a hobby after getting the job? If you pursue your hobby just for one hour per day it will create a great difference?

As long as the height of a human being is up to six feet we accept it easily. But after-attaining six-feet height every extra inch is very costly and it contributes totally a different dimension to one's personality. It is the case with study. Up to graduation, post graduation and Doctoral study, everybody pursue bookish education. However, even after obtaining the doctoral degree how many people continue the study? Most of the doctorates encash their Ph.D. degree for the rest of their lives and gradually they separate themselves from the domain of research and education. Especially in India, even in foreign countries, whenever a person is given an administrative work he is distanced from academic atmosphere. This is highly corroding. Whenever you close your books you are academically dead. Don't accept this academic death. A man should remain a student till the last day of his life. There is no limit to it. The field of education and learning is just like a vast ocean. Irrespective of our qualifications, all of us can be considered as some pebbles in the seashore. We are really very small in comparison to the ocean of knowledge and information. So we should never separate ourselves from this ocean of knowledge. Always we must update our information and tuned with the current happenings in the field of our expertise.

40

Have Little Exercise

Having little exercise everyday is very essential. In the third world countries like India, rarely we see people doing exercise at later ages. We think, it is for the young generation. But we are absolutely wrong. Always we give a common excuse that we don't have time. We have time for everything but not for the exercise. We sleep regularly; we gossip for hours together, we share our feelings and criticize others for a long time but rarely do we find time for exercise. Actually we don't want it, for that we give all these silly excuses. Every human being gets twenty-four hours time. It is up to him how he is utilizing the time. If you visit some park you will find many old people doing exercise. I saw it and initially I was very much impressed. But afterwards I learnt that those old people were diabetic patients and they were taking exercise according to the advice of their doctors. Rarely did they walk half a kilometre everyday in their young age. We the Indians don't even walk hundred metres regularly when we are fit and healthy. We are prone to sedentary life style. We invite diseases by consuming excess food and when we become the victim of some disease like diabetes then at the middle of our life we start exercises. There is a famous English proverb, 'A stitch in time saves nine.' People who start exercise after being sick realize it very much. In western countries, the concept of exercise is very much different. They maintain good figures and for them physical exercise is a regular part of their daily life. In India, we respect a scholar, but most of the scholars are physically unfit and they are not even able to walk properly. You may be a scholar, but only to be a scholar is not enough. You must have an impressive look. If you don't have it then try for it. Good health condition is the prerequisite to be a smart person. You are not supposed to compete in a body-building competition. But you need to devote at least half an hour time for exercise and meditation regularly according to your convenience. It may be in the morning or evening. That is your decision. Take weekly off for one day. But maintain it. Both good and bad things never occur overnight, it takes its due time. When you see a man in very healthy condition at the age of eighty then you praise it. But there must be effort of decades behind this good health. Health is wealth and no opulence of this world can replace a bad health. Your life is in your hand. Once one of my close relatives wanted to give me something. He was very rich and proud of his wealth. He asked me, 'Tell me what do you want'? He kept a blank cheque in front of me and requested me to write the amount. I looked at his pride and laughed in my sleeve. I wrote in the cheque, 'The cost of the tooth which I lost.'

He was shocked. Even if one accumulates the total wealth of the whole world, it can't replace a single tooth, forget about the total health and body. From this you can easily realize the price and importance of a good health. Better late than never. If you are a middle-aged person then also avenues are open in front of you. Start today. Don't delay. Procrastination has become a part and parcel of your life. It is a vice.

Once one great personality was asked, 'Why winter is the season of sin'? He explained it in a very logical way. He stated, 'Inactivity is sin and during winter we become inactive. For that winter is the season of sin.' How beautiful the explanation is! So keep yourself engaged in exercise at least for half an hour everyday.

41

Be Truly Educated

True education and qualification doesn't have any relation. Even a person with doctorate degree may not be educated in real sense; on the contrary an illiterate person may be truly educated. True education means sharing of knowledge, not to have the boasting of the knowledge. True education can be compared with deep-water fish. Small fishes are always in a disturbing state very near to the water surface in a pond. But the deep-water fishes are bigger in size and little chaotic. They rarely come near the surface. Truly educated means a person with due gravity who can manage the show. A truly educated person never exhibits his degrees on his visiting card. True education is a completely ego less state of mind.

Let me tell you a story. Once a faculty of Regional Engineering College, Durgapur went to IIT-Kharagpur for delivering some lecture to the students of post graduation. After delivering his talk, he was returning from Kharagpur to Kolkata by a local train. He was the head of the department of Chemical Engineering and he was well known for his good nature and substantial research in the field of visco-elastic fluid. In the train they were returning to their home in Kolkata. All these students were very egoistic for being the IITians, from top to bottom they were wearing the logo of IIT. They had caps where the symbol of IIT was embossed. They had shirts with the logo of 'IIT Kharagpur'. Apart from that for displaying to the common public, they were carrying the laboratory journals of their institute. Those boys were occupying seats opposite to this gentleman. After sometime they had some technical argument about the subject of Fluid Mechanics and they had different opinions about the visco-elastic fluid. Suddenly the professor interfered in their discussion and said, 'My boys, may I say something about your doubt'? One boy was very aggressive. He replied, 'Sir we are IITians. What you would like to say? You are a common person travelling in the local train at this age and how do you expect us to listen to your suggestion. Sir, we are from IIT Kharagpur. An ordinary passenger like you can't teach us.' The comment of the boy hurt the professor but he wasn't angry. However, he didn't disclose his identity to those students. After that the professor didn't say a single word and the boys also left that compartment. While getting down at the Howrah station, the professor could see one of the boys and called him. The professor gave him an envelope and requested him to hand over it to the head of the department of Chemical Engineering of IIT-Kharagpur. The boy smelled something, but didn't ask anything.

After returning to IIT, the same letter was handed over to the HOD of Chemical Engineering Department; and just after few minutes the HOD called all those five boys who were travelling that day in the train. The HOD told them, 'My boys, I am proud of you people. There is great praise from Dr. Sen who noticed your discussion about visco-elastic fluid. He is the pioneer in the field of visco-elastic fluid. Even I was his student in Jadavpur University.' The HOD didn't know the actual episode how Dr. Sen was insulted by one of the boys. The students became speechless by this polite gesture of that great master. This is the classic example of true education. True education gives you the power of sustainability and power to forgive the juniors.

42

Have Your True Vocation

One must have his true vocation. Once one gentleman commented, 'Labour is the gateway to success.' Then his friend rectified him and told, 'I do agree labour is the gateway to success but it must be coupled with proper decision.' If your decision is wrong then in spite of being intelligent you will be lost forever. There are many brilliant candidates who lost the total potential due to wrong stream of study. In my native place there was a very intelligent boy. Both his parents were professors in reputed colleges. The boy was exceptionally brilliant but his main inclination was towards arts. He had staunch love for literature. At the age of sixteen, he became a prodigy for his exceptional knowledge and writing skills. He was equally comfortable both in Bengali and English. He passed the tenth examination with flying colours, in all the languages he scored highest marks in the board. His command over English was unbelievable. He took admission in a famous junior college in Kolkata. He successfully completed his Higher Secondary examination and appeared for the Joint Entrance Examination. He was selected both in Engineering and Medical science. But he wanted to pursue his career in language and preferably he wanted to explore the horizon of English literature. But his parents didn't allow him to pursue career in literature. They forced him to take admission in Medical science and under compulsion he took admission in the famous Medical College of Kolkata. After attending the college, he lost the complete interest in studies and started bunking lectures. He was a very popular student. Many of his batchmates took admission in other reputed colleges like Scottish Church College and Presidency College of Kolkata. He used to spend the whole day in the famous coffee house of Kolkata with his friends. His friend circle was a good combination of intelligent boys and girls from various walks of the city. Gradually, he was addicted to drugs. His mother used to give him good amount of pocket money and the boy used to spend them in gambling. By gambling he used to earn good amount and he used to spend that amount in drugs and prostitution. Money brings vices and for that boy, the excess money was the main problem.

Ultimately, the boy failed in the first year of MBBS and became utterly frustrated. After that he was confined in home due to utter depression. Then he took eight long years to complete his medical degree. After that he didn't get chance in any of the postgraduate course due to his less mark and bad academic records during under graduation. He joined a small hospital in the suburb of Kolkata. A brilliant career was crushed under the grinding wheel of depression and failure. All his ordinary friends excelled in their career. This is life. Truth is stranger than fiction. So choice of vocation is very important. Ordinary students are less sensitive. They can adjust in any profession, but the extraordinary students are very sensitive. If weeds are not nurtured, even then they will grow; but if a rose plant is not given the proper manure it will certainly wilt within no time. Same thing happens with good students. So one should think twice before selecting his vocation. Because choice of vocation is the pivot on which the whole life rests forever.

43

Have Correct Practice

There is a proverb in English, 'Practice makes a man perfect.' But have you ever felt if anyone practises wrong thing then what will be the result of it. There are millions of students and many of them study sincerely, still very few of them become successful in life. So pursuing correct practice is very much important. Let me share one of my personal experiences with you.

There was a student in the College of Engineering, Pune. In spite of hard work, he never scored well in the examination. I noticed that and one day I called that boy. I asked him, 'You are more sincere than most of the students of the class, but why you are unable to score.' He replied, 'I don't know, I can only tell you that I score good marks in the theory part in the examination but whenever problem comes I get nearly zero or zero mark. The answers obtained by me rarely matches with my friends who get the correct answers most of the times.' I got the clue. I guessed he must be doing some serious error while calculating in the calculator and it must be creeping into all the papers related to Mathematics. He must be doing it unknowingly. Then for testing him I gave him a problem of Fluid Mechanics and told him to solve it in front of me.

The first thing which I observed was that he was using the calculator in a too complicated way, he was simultaneously carrying out five to six activities in spite of going step by step. I don't want to go to the technical details of the operating style of a scientific calculator. Then I found a very dangerous thing. I found him totally ignorant about expressing the power of ten in calculator by using the exponential button. For expressing hundred, we write as 1 exp 02, and it results into 100. He used to write 10 exp 02 for expressing 100. So in spite of 100 he used to get 1000. So in all his calculations, the answer used to vary to a great extent. Because he was unknowingly committing a mistake and the result was ten times of the expected digits after calculation. In case of fraction, his results were also ten times more than the desired and actual results. I found it and counselled him. He was so happy that I can't express it in words. For this silly reason, he was unable to score right from the first semester of the first year to the mid of the second year.

Why practice always doesn't pay is very much clear from this example.

So before you practise any thing; ask yourself whether you are pursuing correct practice or not.

44

Don't Extinguish the Candle

Always we celebrate birthdays with cake and candles. It is a very common scene. Before cutting the cake we blow off all the candles. Why to extinguish the candles? I would like to share my personal experience. It was the year 1992 and the place was Jalgaon. My daughter was just one year old and we were celebrating her first birthday. Few faculties and friends were present. One of my very close friends was present there with me. He is Dr. R. P. Singh. He was a faculty of Mathematics Department and he was very famous for his distinguished personality and outspoken nature. Before the cake was cut, all the children and ladies present over there, forced the small child to blow the candle off, but my daughter was really not in a position to understand the meaning of their instruction. Then suddenly, Dr. Singh told in Hindi, *'Are rahane do dada, kyun bacche ko diya bujhane ke liye majboor kar rahe hein yey log. Janamdin ki khusi to diya jalnemehi rahega na!'* I was really touched by his suggestion. I too felt instantly that it was nothing but an idiocy to extinguish the candle. I prevented them from forcing her. Then the cake was cut and all the pieces were distributed. Light is energy, light is life. Why to extinguish it? So I too appeal, let the birthday candle burn till the wax is there. Let there be light till the end of the birthday. Do you get me or not? Please try once. You will realize it. Please don't consume the whole cake. Keep one or two pieces for the guest who may come late in the evening.

45

One Plus One Equal to One

The name of the chapter seems to be very funny. But once I explain it, you will certainly agree with me. In a dark room, one fellow was sitting. Then one person came to the room with a child. The child was asked by the first person whether he loves his father or mother. The child was confused. Then the question was further complicated when it was asked whom he loves more. The child couldn't answer. The fellow who was sitting in that dark room was very crooked and cynic. He was a sadist and he was expressing his frustration. The child was being harassed for nothing. The person who accompanied the child became angry. Then suddenly he went outside and within couple of minutes returned with a candle. Rays of light were being emitted from the candle. After five minutes again he went outside and returned with another candle. He kept both the candles in front of the cynic person and asked him to guess which candle produced more light. The cynic person was highly confused. He answered, 'It is totally impossible to guess and say how much light is produced by each candle. Because when both the candles are present together there is overlapping of lights from each of them.' The second person answered that is the reason the child couldn't answer your question, because parents are just like two candles. Love of each parent gets superimposed and that too also nothing else than love. There are some sectors of life where you can't differentiate the quantity. Can you say where the river is ending and the sea is starting? Can you say where the day is ending and the night is starting? They are in the process of transition. You can peel a banana but if you try to peel out the mysteries of the nature then it will be dangerous. There are places where one plus one doesn't produce two, it becomes one. Because they belong to the same thing like the love of the parents.

46

Unhappy People are Always Rude

I have seen and experienced many rude people in my life. According to the theory of Psychology, rudeness is nothing but the manifestation of suppression of sex. In eastern countries we see more numbers of rude people. Our culture is different. In the countries where free sex is allowed, there you will find comparatively less numbers of rude people. Officially a person can have only one partner and in most of the cases there physical compatibility doesn't match. In the Indian context, for many couples it is a forced living together under one roof. In India, we see sex from a different angle. It's more a thing to suppress than to express. Sex education is a great problem in our country. Millions of people are being affected by AIDS and by 2020 whether India will be superpower or not that I can't say, but from the view point of AIDS certainly it will be one of the top rankers in the world.

If I discuss a case study, then it will be clear. In Pune there is a Bengali family. It is a joint family. It consists of seven members. The old father and mother stay with their elder son, two daughter-in-laws and two grandsons. The younger son of the couple died of

Leukaemia just after three years of the marriage. The elder son is placed in a public sector undertaking. The wife of the elder son is also working with an airlines company. The old couple is still romantic. The younger daughter-in-law is from a poor family and is a housewife. She had to follow the orthodoxy of a Hindu widow. She can't take any non-vegetarian food but she has to cook for all other family members. Question of remarriage doesn't arise. Her age is only twenty-seven. Since the last three years, she is living the dry life of a widow. In front of her other senior members of the family are enjoying a comfortable sex life. In this context, if she behaves in an erratic or rude way then who is responsible? We people point our finger to an irritated nature of an orthodox widow, but have we ever tried to place ourselves in her place? In most of the cases, the widows are not orthodox; orthodoxy is imposed on them. Even after sixty three years of independence, we couldn't be modern. We are only externally modern, but most of the minds are filled with old superstitions and dogmas. The modernization achieved by us can be called apparent modernization. How many people are there who gladly accept a widow as their wife? Very few. We are only qualified in paper.

Unhappy people are always rude. Whenever you see a rude person please go deep. Go to his childhood.

In Pune, there is a famous engineering college. One senior most faculty of that college is very rude and negative minded. I personally witnessed the deeds of that gentleman many times. He is highly negative minded and depressed at core. I tried to vindicate the reason behind this sadist attitude. Afterwards, I came to know that during his childhood and boyhood, he was severely tortured by his father and he was the victim of mental harassment. Today his deeds are nothing but the cumulative result of the torture sustained by him. It is like Black body (detail discussion of Black body is beyond the scope of this book, because it belongs to the highly mathematical subject named Heat Transfer). So if there is some cause behind this rudeness, we should try to find out and solve it. If it is possible then it is well and good. If not possible then there is no remedy to it. It is easy to give lectures like the politicians. Because they promise but don't implement their promises. Politicians even promise bridges without a river. But in real life it is not so easy to promise. There is a saying, 'Nothing is impossible.' It's only a saying. There are many impossible things in this world. We can only try to solve maximum numbers of problems, but some mysteries will be certainly remained for the next generation.

47

Enjoy the Beauty, don't Capture it

I visited many places, many sea beaches, many resorts and many hill stations. Everywhere I found a common thing. I found people busy in capturing the photographs rather than enjoying the beauty of it. Once I had been to the famous caves of Ajanta in Maharashtra of India. There was a tourist group from an European country. All of them had movie camera with them. That time the culture of handycam and digital camera was not so popular. I found all of them shooting continuously for hours. I introduced myself and frankly asked them, 'Are you not preoccupied with this shooting? I found all of you shooting continuously for the last one hour. Probably it is your first visit to Ajanta caves. If you do so, when will you enjoy the beauty of the famous paintings by our ancestors?' They kept mum and I didn't get any satisfactory reply from anyone of them.

Once I had been to the famous hill station of Mahabaleshwar in India. I witnessed the same thing. Around the dusk we reached the famous sunset point. Except me all the members of our group were busy in capturing the photograph of the setting sun. I was the only odd man out. I was being drenched by the crimson beams of the setting sun. A person who was busy in taking photograph wasn't enjoying the beauty. Because his mind was blocked to take the best photograph. Nowadays due to the revolution of handycam, digicam and Internet one can take thousands of pictures and edit them afterwards. I know people, who take thousands of photographs in each visit, then they simply transfer those photographs from the camera to their personal computers or laptop. Rarely are they viewed by anyone in the future. It's a typical mania. You may have food, but you are not supposed to eat always. When you really feel hungry then you have it. The meaning of any excursion is not taking the photographs. God gifted us pair of eyes. How many of us are aware of it? Have you ever enjoyed the beauty of a butterfly over green grass in a winter evening? Stand for a while, be calm and look around the garden. You will certainly get a new meaning of life. Don't be preoccupied in capturing the beauty, try to feel it and assimilate the conversation of the nature. Be relaxed. Only relaxed state of mind is the prerequisite for entering the world of happiness and peace. Because this relaxed state is free from all kinds of preoccupation.

48

Don't Give Big References

Giving big references is a very bad habit of the people. People always give big references and try to enjoy a pseudo status. One of my neighbours in West Bengal was a lower division clerk and his brother-in-law was the General Manager of Kolkata telephones. In those days there was no private telecom companies. So Department of Post and Telegraph had monopoly. That neighbour always used to talk of his brother-in-law, though the brother-in-law never even came to his house, though my neighbour's wife was his real sister. In any occasion his wife used to visit her brother in his giant quarters in the city of Kolkata. Even his children used to go to their maternal uncle's place during the holidays.

Bur rarely we give the reference of a relative or friend who is unsuccessful in life. Even every college is boasting of the alumni who are celebrities. Let the alumni say that he is from this college. The institutes are giving hype to the celebrity alumni. Most of them were very ordinary students but somehow they made good amount of money. On the contrary, the real topper of a batch must be rotting as a faculty in some remote university of the country. Institutes are begging for funds. Though there are cases where out of their own love the alumni donated money. There is reverse picture also. The concerned Principal of reputed institutes visited the alumni but got very poor response.

Before giving references we must ask who is benefited. Most of the times the person who is referred doesn't even bother for us. Once one poor Bengali lady was there in my native place. Her husband used to talk to us in the teashop where I used to pass my evening time during the days of my post graduation. One day the gentleman requested me to take the private tuition of his daughter. They were poor. One day I visited them and talked to the girl. Then I decided to teach her and started taking the tuition. The girl was not brilliant. When my fee was asked I told them to give me Rs. 125 per month. It was 1988. After teaching for one month I got my first remuneration. The gentleman's brother was a renounced lawyer in Kolkata. He never bothered for his poor brother. But that famous lawyer didn't sacrifice the part of the house that he got as his share of the ancestral property. Then I continued my tuition and they couldn't give me the fees for three months. Seeing their condition I could not want it. The girl was anaemic. I thought if I had helped them it would have been better. But due to my crisis my hands were tied. Financial crunch is a gift, which I got by birth. So I accepted it with a sporting spirit. Because with my philosophical mind-set it is difficult to earn and I don't want it at the cost of compromising my beliefs.

While teaching that girl one day her mother asked me a very important question. She asked, 'Can you tell, why poor people are heckled for nothing and rich people are flattered without any reason'? It was a beautiful question. Today at the mid stream of my life from my vast experience if I want to search the answer then I would say it is the in-built human nature to mock at the poor and to be submissive in front of richness.

So you be great, don't give reference of a great person. Have your own identity. Let it be small but let it be original and authentic.

49

Want Substantial Things from God

Let me share a beautiful incident with all of you. Once in the Sunday morning I was going through some technical journals. Suddenly someone pressed the door bell. I opened the door and found a young couple standing. They were smart and good-looking. I invited them and requested them to have their seat. Then I came to know they are working on behalf of an NGO for the orphans. They came for collecting some donations. There were various categories of donations. One may sponsor a child for the whole year or half of the year. One may sponsor a child partly. As for example one may sponsor only the education expense of a child or one may sponsor the clothes and food expenditure of a child. It is up to the sponsors. One can sponsor more than one child. For sponsoring a child one need not be very rich, but one requires a truly rich mind. Generally I observed that whenever people come to know that someone came for donation they don't even talk to them. They possess a phobia from the people who come in the name of donation. This is bad. At least one must treat them properly and one should listen to them. They are having good background and working for a noble cause. We must not shut our doors on their face.

I offered them water and tea and discussed with them. It is observed that very ordinary people with average financial background sponsored a child. On the contrary very rich people didn't sponsor even a single child.

I was ready to sponsor a child for six months. Then they asked me to mention a name that should be referred by the child during prayer. Generally people give the names of their beloved family members. I came to know most of the donors gave the name of their children. That means since the donation is given for that those orphans will take the name of the children of those donors while praying to God. Indirectly they will pray for the donors' children as a gesture. It is a mark of gratefulness. I simply laughed. I told, 'Even the orphans are also kids. Why they should pray for my child? She is O.K. On the contrary they are in problem.' I requested them not to take any names from my family. I want the child to pray for his best friend in the orphanage. I never wanted materialistic things from God. Before my daughter was born I visited the famous temple of Saibaba in Shirdi. That is the substantial thing I wanted from God.

50

Earning Money and Spending Life

Earning money is important but it is not the only thing in life. You may earn money later, but you won't get back the today, which you are losing permanently for chasing after money. Money is the petrol of life's engine. It is required. But it is not welcome at the cost of personal peace and pleasure. There was a famous structural engineer. He used to earn millions of dollars per month. He had to roam across the world frequently. He was obsessed with money and work. For money he was ready to leave everything. Due to heavy work, addiction of tobacco and alcohol, disturbed lifestyle he became impotent. After marriage he couldn't give anything to his wife. He was not ready to take even treatment. Because he didn't have time to visit the doctors and follow their prescriptions. He used to stay with his wife in Mississippi. One night after returning from office he found a letter in the kitchen platform. The wife abandoned him and went away with another person. After few days the wife sent a notice of the lawyer for divorce. She wanted unconditional divorce and didn't highlight the weak point of that person and didn't want any sort of alimony.

The gentleman got the divorce but he played a mischief. Since his wife didn't disclose his weak point, for that he took the undue advantage of it. He married a very beautiful lady and the difference of their age was more than twenty. The age of his wife was approximately half of his age.

This lady was adamant and she was having severe sexual urge. Within no time she found the man was unable to do anything. She straightaway consulted her lawyer and filed a case of clear cheating. The structural consultant started consulting his lawyer and for face saving he had to spend a lot. In one side he ran after money and on the other way he had to spend money for his misdeeds. He had everything except peace and friend. Everybody used to hate him. Even his family members used to hate him. He didn't have even good terms with his parents and siblings. For him the main mission of life was to earn money and see it. He hardly spent money for some noble cause. Once one sub-ordinate of his office pasted a small paper in the door. There it was written, 'Save money, see it and die.' It was really applicable to this person.

But that small chit couldn't influence him in a positive way. He was very rigid and throughout his life he was equally obstinate. He died at the age of seventy-eight. He had huge properties. But he didn't give any clear directives before his death about the heir of his properties. Even his second wife left him. He didn't have any legal heir. So ultimately the total property worth billions of dollars was ceased by the Government. This becomes the pathetic end of these types of people. The best use of money lies in the proper spending of it. So earn money but don't spend your life for earning money.

Long back I saw a movie. The basic theme of the movie was the unceasing struggle of a couple to purchase an apartment in a posh locality of a city. Initially when they tried to purchase it was beyond their reach. Then at the cost of all small pleasures of life they started saving money. Even they stopped taking newspapers. Initially the lady was a housewife. Then she joined a company as a receptionist. By there struggle they saved money for ten years at the cost of their youth. After ten years when they went to purchase the apartment they again failed. Because by that time the price was three-fold. So they lost both. Neither they could afford the apartment nor could they enjoy their youth. So please be careful. For money and materialistic comforts don't spend your life. Every moment of your life is unique. They come only once. You can't store them. So make the proper use of your life.

51

Care for People

In this chapter I would like to share with you a great experience of my life. Till date I am having confusion about the way people worship the God. Generally in India people who belong to the Hindu religion visit several temples and during any religious occasion the frequency of their visit increase a lot. I used to visit the temple of 'SANI' (Saturn) in Saturdays. In the Hindu religion Saturn is considered as a very powerful God and it decides the destiny of a person. This is a common belief. In the Hindu astrology, they say in your horoscope if Saturn is bad and all other planets are in good position still you are bound to fail miserably in life. It is the deciding planet of one's fate. Most of the people go to the Saturn temple out of fear not out of respect or love. It is believed that Saturn is a scrupulous observer and it becomes very happy if it finds you donating some amount to some poor people. It likes charity. Generally people go to the Saturn temple every Saturday, pour oil on the head of the God, and have seven rounds around the idol. They place garlands made of some special leaf, place broken coconuts, light the ghee lamps and place some small or big amount in the donation box kept at the corner of the temple.

Every Saturday I used to visit the temple near my colony, stand at a corner and minutely observe the behaviour of the people in a very scrupulous way. Once one gentleman wanted to donate rupees fifty in the donation box, but seeing that his wife was shocked. Her statement is still engraved in my mind. She told, 'What are you doing? Are you a fool? Give five rupees. If God gives money then you give whatever you want; I won't mind. I wanted you to be a rich person and today I wanted your promotion from God.' This is the level of the common people. Even with their God they possess a give and take relation. This needs to be changed. They donate in the donation box but before that think twice, even thrice. But they seldom give a single pie to the beggars and handicapped who wait for some donation outside the temple. The numbers of beggars and lepers are directly proportional to the importance of the temple and popularity of the God. In India after visiting any temple if the demands of the common people are fulfilled then that God gains popularity and it is treated as a very powerful and co-operative God.

Now I would like to say what I do. There are lakhs of people to take care of God, but there are few to take care of them who are really needy. I used to give ten rupees to a handicapped beggar who used to come every Saturday in front of the Saturn temple. One Saturday I was tired and my mind wanted rest. But I had to go. God was not waiting for me, but the beggar was waiting for me. If I would not have gone then that poor beggar would have waited for me till the late night (as long the temple remained open). I couldn't prevent myself from visiting. Because I realized God within that poor beggar.

52

You are a Pendulum between Smile and Tears

Once I attended one conference. The theme of the conference was 'How to maintain a perfect lifestyle.' There were many good speakers. Out of them one speaker was extraordinary for his oratory skill. While delivering talk once he commented, 'You are a pendulum between smile and tears.' It is absolutely correct. One can't expect happiness in all the moments of life. Similarly one can't be sad everytime. Life is a mixture of joyful incidence and sad happenings. In a family when a death takes place then all the family members become morose. In the same family when a child is born all the family members become happy. So life is a mixture of both. As we can't stop the pendulum, we can't stop the happenings of our life. They are just like in-built programmes. You can't avoid them.

There is a chapter in the subject of Fluid Mechanics in Engineering studies. The name of the chapter is 'Boundary Layer Theory'. The content of the chapter is highly technical and beyond the scope of this non-fiction. But in this chapter there is a very important topic called separation. It is proved scientifically that at the most separation can be delayed, but not avoided. Similarly in life we can't get rid of all the sad happenings. We may take care, we may be disciplined. But luck will play its own role. Though often we say we don't believe in luck and some people say that luck controls only one per cent of our fate. These are all irrelevant. Actually luck is everything. If you are born in a good and educated family that can be also considered as your luck. Nothing can be done regarding that. We don't have any control on those things, which are thrust on us. But we can beautify those things, which are in our possession. Let us accept both tears and smiles. It will help us in leading a good life.

53

Don't do too Many Things at a Time

Most of the people try to do too many things at a time. Once one teacher suggested a very good thing to his students. He suggested, 'Never go for more than one book at your undergraduate level, just read one good book. It will serve your purpose.'

If you follow his suggestion then you will realize it. Now a days in the cities we find kids who are jack of all trades. There are kids who go for sports in the morning and after attending the school, in the evening they go for music and fine arts classes. Why to encumber them with so much loads? There is a limit to everything. In reality it practically takes the whole life to be the expert in one field. Forget about other fields. If you see an Olympic winner you would see that he or she must have devoted whole life and the total energy for the sports and games. On the contrary, if you try to explore all the fields then there is a possibility that you will not be successful in any field and the total efforts taken by you will be of no use. Let me give a very good example. All of us know that lenses are used to converge the rays of light. If you hold a paper below the lens in the sunshine then after some time due to concentrated heat the paper will catch fire. But while doing it if you move your hands here and there the paper will not catch fire. Do you get me or not? I want to say that you must have a fixed direction to be successful in life. Even if you want to be a jack-of-all-trades it will do, but at least try to be master of one.

54

Meaningful Life is the Meaning of Life

If there is no meaning in your life then the life becomes meaningless. The meaning of life must be understood properly. We get only one life. Most of us actually waste seventy to eighty per cent of our life in useless activities like lethargy, gossiping, criticizing others etc. I am in the teaching profession for so many years. Generally in undergraduate and postgraduate level professors get maximum teaching loads of 2-3 hours per day. The total span of duty is eight hours. Randomly if we take a survey then we would find that a faculty gets at least fifty per cent time totally free for doing creative activities. But generally they don't go for that. If it's an in campus job then after the lectures they return to their quarters and take rest. Even in NITs and IITs, I saw faculties enjoying post-pandrial nap. Once the lunchtime is over most of the faculties feel drowsy and they consume tea and coffee for many times. They gossip too much. Mostly they criticize each other in the absence of other faculties. Is it life or hell? By this way they pass thirty to thirty five years of their life. Most of them lose interest in life and somehow drag their life. Due to their cynic nature they are neither liked by the students nor by the family members. In spite of having potential they are corroded and they lead a meaningless life.

So to fill your life with glorious activities you need to pursue positive activities. Be positive. Be involved in creative activities. At least help people. I know people are bad; it's a sad, bad and mad world. But you don't be like them. At least you try to be good. By your good behaviour you may influence ten and those ten may influence a mass of hundred.

Rome was not built in a day. A positive-minded person is the only solution to change this depressed world. Influencing others in the right way is very important. So do such things, which will help you to have a meaningful life.

55

Be a Small Star, Don't be an Eclipsed Sun

In this world, you must have your own identity. I found many people boasting of their relations. There is a common trend in the society that we give only those references who are in big posts and positions. It is not only applicable to families, even it is applicable to institutes. Every institute gives the references of those alumni who are very well known and rich. This is a very common human tendency. Some people get pseudo pleasure by mentioning about relatives who are in good position.

There was a couple from West Bengal. The husband was a clerk but his father-in-law was a district and session judge. His wife always used to give the reference of her father. She was somewhat ashamed of her husband's position. He appeared for IAS examination. His wife and in-laws were very hopeful. But he couldn't pass it. From that very day his wife lost interest in him. It was his first and last chance. So he remained as a clerk for long time and even lost interest in departmental examination for promotion to the cadre of officers. After a decade, he cleared the departmental exam and was promoted to the next higher post. He is still there. However, he is frustrated with his life. The friends and colleagues who were inferior to him excelled him in professional life. He remained as a diamond in dust. Still he is energetic, active and creative even after being an octogenarian. He is having a very close family relation with me.

People go on quoting references but they rarely do something positive. By continuously quoting others' reference they feel privileged.

They are the failures who give others' references. Successful person does not need anybody's reference. Some people feel happy by accompanying celebrities. There is a famous industrialist in India who became industrialist by default. But he is not happy. He couldn't be a celebrity by his qualities. He always prefers to be accompanied by film stars and cricketers. Even that could not give him the status of a celebrity. Because he doesn't have any inner quality which can bring him fame. We often forget one thing that shadow is the by-product of an object; it can't be the object. Similarly company of big people can never make you big. It is always preferable to be a small star than to be a dead planet. A star may be small but it has its own light. On the other hand, the planets are big but they are at the mercy of Sun's light. Be independent. Have self-respect and self-faith. Go ahead. The future is yours.

56

Don't Suppress Your Feelings

In today's era, people have become hypocrites. They are even teaching their children to be like them. At times, parents and guardians encourage their children to tell lies to guardians or parents. Unknowingly, the child is learning how to tell lies and how to pretend in front of guests and strangers. Because of pretentions we suppress our true self, real emotions and feelings.

I would like to tell about an incident. During our college days we used to organise a grand feast every month. Sometimes our rector used to come. In one of the feasts, rector and principal came with their families. The boys were very shy and when the dinner started all of them took very little food for showing the courtesy. Actually most of them were heavy eaters. But someone told them not to behave like gluttons in front of professors. I too observed them and joined them. I was famous for my outspoken nature right from my childhood. I told the Principal, 'Sir they are pretending. After your departure they will again come to the line and will take double amount of food.' The principal was surprised but he understood the whole matter. He laughed and said, 'My boys, enjoy the dinner, I too was a student of this college and nearly three decades ago, I was in the same hostel, my room number was 302 of the last block. It was the last but one room of the top floor. It was the 'D' wing. I had not forgotten my college days. During our time there used to be a great competition of how many sweets one can take.'

The moment he stopped, the boys came out of the veil of shame and started behaving in a normal way. The competition started and the student who stood first consumed thirty-seven pieces of sweets. Initially he was suppressing his greed. Once he came out of it; he enjoyed the grand feast.

57

Save but Spend Too

It is very important to save money in life, but at the same time one must spend for the necessity. A man is known by the habit of his spending. If you give same amount of money to ten different people each of them will spend it in different ways. Saving is important, but there are people who save money at the cost of life. They sacrifice even small pleasures of life for saving money. When my cousin brother's wife became pregnant, she had to go to a doctor in Kolkata for some consultation as it was the case of advance pregnancy. It was difficult for her to travel such a long distance and travelling by public transport was risky in that stage. She requested my brother to avail a private taxi. But my brother was very thrifty. He was determined to go by public transport only. Ultimately he declined the request of his wife and forced her to go by local train to Howrah station. He had a plan to go by some bus from Howrah station. In Howrah station, the train entered in the evening and there was tremendous rush from the opposite side. The people who were supposed to travel to the suburban areas started getting into the train before it stopped. My brother told his wife to get down. While getting down she faced an accident. There was a banana skin in the platform. She slipped and immediately she was rushed to the hospital. The doctor could save her life but could not save the child. For saving few rupees, my brother had to give a tremendous penalty. When my sister-in-law came to know about it she lost her mental balance. Because she was totally prepared to be a mother. Her whole system was ready to accept the motherhood. What a tragedy! She had to go through the complete course of a delivery to remove the dead child. The child was a beautiful girl.

In life you need not go for extravaganza, but you must spend where it is really required. During critical time if you don't spend then your earning loses its meaning. So save but spend too. Spend judiciously and practically.

58

Have Two Ice cream

'You may not be able to afford two Mercedes, but see that you are mentally able enough to enjoy two ice-creams. Your mind must not be eclipsed by misery and min-minded attitude.'

– Arati Mukhopadhyay

I got this teaching right at my childhood when my mother used to counsel me. She never wanted her children to be thrifty. She wanted her children to live their life to the fullest. Really in Indian scenario, it becomes difficult even for an officer to afford a car by honest means. So question of possessing two cars doesn't arise. Forget about Mercedes. But one can easily afford two ice creams. You may think what is the co-relation between ice cream and Mercedes. I have seen many rich people who are thrifty at core. They possess big apartments; big cars, big bungalows but seldom they gift a balloon to their child from the core of their heart. It is unfortunate. This is the irony of life. Knowingly or unknowingly everyday we are approaching the end of our life.

Most of the times people lead a life, which is controlled by the famous proverb 'Penny wise, Pound foolish.' This is an absolutely wrong approach. I am an Indian by birth. Neither I believe in the concept of citizenship nor in the concept of nationality. But here, people are poor and their lifestyle is not high. Their thinking process requires a change and modification. It is very difficult to make them understand that by consuming food you can't be poor. People become beggar overnight by diseases. Only medical expenses can drag a person to footpath unless he is medically insured. So whenever after having one ice cream mind wants the second one; go for it, don't look at your wallet. The second ice cream won't make you poor.

59

Management by a Poor Boy

Management has become the most preferred and sought after branch of study. But thirty years ago it was not that popular. But during those days, I saw my friend to adopt management and it was nothing but crisis management. He was very poor and he didn't have papers to write. So he used to collect old calendars from his neighbourhood and used to solve problems in the backside of the calendar by blue pen. After using blue pen, he would use the same paper and would write with green pen and then again he would use the same piece of paper with red ink. Necessity is the mother of invention and the poverty taught him management. He didn't even know that he was applying the practical aspects of management at that tender age. On one hand poor people apply the science of Management unknowingly and on the other hand, the rich people go for management studies but they are unable to manage their life due to their voluptuous attitudes.

Let me give one more example. In our NIT hostel, there was a very poor boy. Due to poverty it was very difficult for him to have tiffin in the evening. Because college hostel used to give breakfast, lunch and dinner. But there was no provision for evening tiffin.

That boy used to keep his lunch and he used to wait up to 3.00 p.m. He followed the procedure so that in the evening he doesn't feel hungry. These are the true incidents observed by me in my life. This is real struggle. He is well-off now and his children can't even imagine of the quantum of struggle through which their father had to go. With time everything changes.

60

Don't Count Money

Counting money is a disease. One should count money once or twice a day. I know people who count money now and then. After purchasing even some small amount of grocery, they count all the money in their wallet. These are all preoccupations and preoccupation is the sole cause of stress. I know one gentleman. He didn't believe any of his family members. While sleeping he used to keep the key of his cupboard under his pillow and everyday before sleeping, he used to count the total amount of money in the cupboard.

The family members were very unhappy with this cynic person. One day, they decided to play some mischief. After he slept his elder son gently removed the key from the side of his pillow and opened the cupboard. In spite of taking some money from his stored wealth, he added five hundred rupees. Next morning after getting up as usual he counted all the money and said nothing. But he was under stress. It never happened before, everybody in the house watched his body language. Whole day, the gentleman didn't spend anything and repeatedly counted the money. But he couldn't solve the mystery. Then he thought it was his mistake. But he didn't disclose it.

After couple of days, in a night when the man was in deep sleep then again his elder son took the key, opened the cupboard and placed ten notes of five hundred rupees. Next morning the gentleman saw it and thought it was God sent. How idiot people can be! Without saying anything to anyone he went to the nearby temple. After worshipping the God and offering him some money, he returned and announced that last night he got five thousand rupees from God.

When the truth was told, he was not ready to believe it. Noone could convince him. He was a sceptic. Even in his dream he could never think that someone can give money. That retired man was psychologically derailed and admitted to Hospital. While going to the hospital he carried the key. He didn't even believe his wife. Due to psycho-somatic problem and high blood sugar, he was seriously ill and went to deep coma. He never returned from the coma. He left this world within few days. After his death his family members opened the cupboard and all the stored wealth was donated to the poor people. They realized that it was impossible to digest the wealth left by him. This is the end of money-minded people.

61

Bitter and Better

Generally something, which is bitter, is better in the long run. You can take several examples. Right from scolding of the guardians and teachers to the vaccination for typhoid. All are bitter and painful. But in the long run they pay us. The guardians and teachers scold us for our benefits only. But during that span of time we become angry with them. But sometime later in life we truly realize that it was for our benefit only. I remember a teacher. He used to scold us and even he used to beat the students in our school days. The boys were extremely unhappy with him. The said teacher is no more but his motivation is still engraved in our mind. He scolded us; he has beaten us for our benefits only. Same is the case with any vaccination programme. All of us have a suppressed fear for taking injection. Most of us are having Trypanophobia. For that most of the times, we postpone the vaccination programme, because we know vaccination means taking injection. It will be followed by swelling and pain. Even the swelling and pain may be coupled with fever also. So we postpone it to get rid of it for one day. But postponement or procrastination is an inbuilt vice within the human character. We must not postpone it.

In the same way, we don't go for bitter gourd. In front of you if bitter gourd juice and pineapple shake are placed, obviously you would prefer the later one. But bitter gourd is very good for the health. Unless a person becomes the victim of Diabetes, he seldom understands the importance of bitter gourd. So it can be concluded that most of the bitter things are better for health and mind. We too know that but we are not ready to accept them. Let's accept them. Because we can't run away from the truth.

62

Don't be an Escapist

Winners have dreams;
Losers have schemes.

Winners see the gains;
Losers see the pain.

Winners see the potential;
Losers see the past.

Winners make it happen;
Losers let it happen.

Winners see possibilities;
Losers see problems.

Winners makes commitments;
Losers makes promises.

Winners are a part of the team;
Losers are apart from the team.

Winner always has a programme
Loser always has an excuse.

Winner says 'Let me do it for you'
Loser says 'That is not my job.'

Winners say 'I must do something'
Losers say 'Something must be done.'

Winner is always a part of the answer
Loser is always a part of the problem.

Winner sees an answer for every problem
Loser sees a problem for every answer.

Winners believe in win/win
Loser believe for them to win, someone has to lose.

Winner says 'It may be difficult but it is possible'
Loser says 'It may be possible but it is too difficult.'

Winner makes a mistake. He says 'I was wrong'
Loser makes a mistake; he says 'It wasn't my fault.'

– Anonymous

Losers are nothing but escapist. From the above lines it is crystal clear that there are hundreds of ways to give excuse. So don't be an escapist. Escapists lack self-respect. Self-respect is the most important thing in life.

63

Don't Bargain Much

Bargaining is good but too much of bargaining is bad. Let me tell you one of my personal experiences. I was in Rourkella with one of my relatives. We went to see a movie in the afternoon and after the movie we were returning. In the road, there were less crowd and a very heavy downpour was awaited. I got an auto rickshaw and told him the destination. He charged rupees twelve. But my relative was senior to me and he was not ready to give him twelve rupees. He was ready to pay only rupees ten. The auto driver was not agreed and at last he was agreed to accept rupees eleven. But my relative was very stubborn. That time I was a college student. I said, 'Why are you bothering for just one rupee. Give him and let us go.' He replied, 'You shut up. You are a mere student. Do you know the value of money? Have you earned a penny in life? Just stop.' Seeing the rage and fury, I stopped but felt insulted. The auto driver also stuck to his decision and ultimately he left.

By that time the rain came and there was no nearby shelter and we didn't have umbrella or raincoat. I was very angry but I had to keep mum. We had to languish in the heavy rain for nearly forty minutes, the frequency of auto rickshaw also reduced. If any auto rickshaw was available they charged twenty to twenty five rupees. The hope to reach the home by spending only rupees ten was crushed totally. Then after being completely drenched, we reached home by walking after one and half hour. I was angry and he was also irritated. I was attacked by severe cold and my relative was attacked by chest pain followed by pneumonia. Within forty-eight hours, he was admitted in a hospital and had to stay there for a complete fortnight. What a terrible penalty we had to give just for one rupee.

There is a reason behind telling this story. You can draw the inference, who is the loser. Certainly the auto driver was not the loser. Because he must have got some other passenger. My relative was the main loser for his rigid nature and I was the victim. Even I could have been also attacked by pneumonia but thanks to my young age and luck. The fun derived out of seeing the picture was totally lost due to that nasty bargaining. Bargaining is good, but if it dampens the pleasure of shopping then it is certainly bad. So don't bargain at the cost of your mental tranquillity and peace.

64

Face the Problem

For solving any problem one needs to face it. It may be an examination, it may be fear of ghost or it may be trauma from injection. The more you avoid it, the more you become preoccupied. Every person has got the fear of death. But either today or tomorrow we need to face it. There is no escape from it. So when we need to face a problem why not to face it boldly and joyously?

Let me give a beautiful example. It was in the year 1984. We were in the second year of Engineering. The semester examination was in full swing. There was a subject named Strength of Materials. It was a core subject for all the students of the second year. It was a mathematical subject and it was considered as one of the hardest subjects of engineering. Suddenly a group of students decided to drop that particular subject because they were not prepared at all. Whenever you surrender there is an apparent relaxation. But afterwards frustration peeps into your mind. Same thing happened there. Whenever a group does some wrong thing they want their group to be strong. So those boys started frightening other boys and in the morning the total number in that group was only fourteen but by the evening it was fifty-eight. Nearly thirty to forty per cent students of Civil and Mechanical Engineering made their mind to drop that examination. They were not preparing for the next paper, but they were in search of new candidates who could be demotivated.

By next morning, the total number in that group reached sixty-three. There was a very ordinary student. He was taciturn and never used to mix up with others. His academic progress was at low ebb. Next day when he was going for the examination this group tried to prevent him from going, but the boy was very stubborn. He didn't listen to them. From the group one boy commented, 'Let him go, he will fail.' The boy got angry and answered, 'I may fail. But if at all I fail I shall fail after facing the examination, but all of you failed even before appearing. You people are cowards, because you have surrendered. You people are not ready to face the problem. You are running away from the problem.'

After the examination, it was found that the question paper was easy as compared to other years. After nearly two months, when the result was published it was noticed that the taciturn boy cleared the subject. Even if this group had studied sincerely then at least fifty to sixty per cent students of that group would have passed because most of them were intelligent. So take this as a lesson. Always you need to face the problem. If you run away from any problem, the problem will not be solved. On the contrary, with each passing day it will be more and more complicated. Whenever anything is delayed it becomes more and more complicated and it becomes really difficult to have the solution after long time. It is wise to face all the problems and jot down the ways to solve it, try it and explore the world of success.

65

Discover Ability in Others

It's a great quality to discover ability in others. He is a true leader who can see the leadership quality in others. There was a professor in the Civil Engineering Department of an engineering college. He was very famous for his simple teaching style and down-to-earth attitude. He was also famous for his approachability. Every year he used to guide a project batch. But he never used to take the top rankers in his batch. He had more than twenty years of teaching experience. He was well aware of the nature of the students. Once he told, 'The top rankers are very good. They can work with hundred per cent efficiency, but if you expect them to take out even ten per cent efficiency out of the project group they can't. They are usually selfish, narrow minded, bookish and they lack vision for going ahead.' He had the ability to find the ability of leadership within some mediocre students and only for that reason his project group was used to consist of mediocre students.

To discover ability in others is not an ordinary thing. Let me share one more incident.

A shooting was in progress for a dance scene in some spot. Suddenly the director watched a child. He was from the nearby slum, and came to see the shooting in the suburb of Mumbai. The director found the child dancing at one corner. Even without any sort of formal training, the child picked up the steps and started dancing. When the choreographer was teaching the steps, the small child scrupulously observed each steps and remembered them quickly. The director observed the child for a long time. He was very much impressed and brought it to the notice of the choreographer. Even she was impressed. They contacted the parents of the child and ultimately he was admitted to a dance school. After a couple of years, that child became one of the famous dancers of the country. If that day the director wouldn't have seen the quality within the child or if he would have ignored it then the poor child would have lost the chance to become a dancer. That's why it is important and praiseworthy to discover ability in others.

66

Undo Your Depression

Nobody on this earth is totally happy. Happiness is a state of mind and it depends on many aspects, viz., your family background, your educational qualification, relation with your siblings, your family liabilities, your financial condition, relation with your spouse, your office atmosphere and several other parameters. It is practically impossible to be successful in all the sphere of life. A person may be in a very high position if the professional front is considered, but he may have strained relation with his spouse. On the other hand, a person may enjoy a very happy family life but can have financial crunch. So one way or the other, every person has to face some sort of difficulties in life.

There are three kinds of people on this earth. The first kind got more than they actually deserve, the second kind received the desired thing and the last kind got less than actually they deserve. In most of the cases, the third kind of people become the victim of depression. There are cases when we see the backbencher of a school became a great entrepreneur in later life and made kingdom and the first boy of the school ended his life as a meagre clerk in a nationalized bank. We often say, get rid of depression. But it's not that easy. There is always some cause behind every depression. If it is a genetic disorder then treatment is required. If it is not genetic then we must vindicate the reason for the depression and if possible we have to uproot the cause of depression.

I would like to share one incident. There was a retired colonel in Kolkata. He had a daughter. The daughter was very jolly and she was married to a banker. Just after marriage, the jolly girl gradually became saturnine and after one year she was totally depressed and returned to her father's house. The colonel was a smart person. He had a very friendly term with his daughter. After enquiry he came to know that the son-in-law was totally impotent and it was incurable. Then he took the decision immediately. He advised her daughter to file the divorce case. There are people who sustain this type of problem for lifetime for the fear of the society. The colonel was a logical person and apart from that he was a loving father. He didn't want his daughter to go astray. Sentiment can't solve all the problems. After a couple of months, the girl got the divorce and was remarried to a major. Presently she is happily staying in Uttaranchal. If the depression can be cured by some act or action it must be adopted. The colonel did the same thing. This is a very elaborative subject.

I would like to narrate one more case. There was a student who loved language. After his schooling, his parents forced him to be a doctor. He took seven years to complete the study of medicine. He got the degree but he didn't have any intention to practise medicine as a profession. Ultimately, he did MBA and afterwards he did Ph.D. in Management Studies. Presently he is a faculty of Management Science. Apart from that he is a columnist in a famous English daily. He did correct thing. During young age due to the pressure of the parents he couldn't do anything. But later he realized that medical profession couldn't produce any amount of success for him. Better late than never. So though late, he decided to pursue MBA.

So if you are depressed then first and foremost thing is to find the cause of depression. If it is curable then go for it. Don't ignore it. Don't waste your life unnecessarily.

67

Experience and Experiment

The basic difference between experience and experiment is that experiments are done but experience is felt. Experience is one step ahead of experiment. In our college days, we performed practicals in Chemistry. Most of us had to face one or two minor accidents in the Chemistry laboratory. Sometimes our hands get burn in the flame of Bunsen burner, sometimes we face little injuries while pouring acids etc. One might have forgotten all the practicals carried out by him long back, but rarely one forgets the experience of the accidents. This is engraved in one's mind. Generally in life, experience is more important than experiments. For that most of the times we give values to the advice of the seniors, though they may be less qualified. Paper qualification is one thing, and the experience of one's life is another thing. Generally, the elderly persons are respected, because they have seen the world more than us.

In the city of Kolkata, a man was going to office. He didn't take the umbrella. It was a sunny day, but it was the time of rainy season. While leaving the house he met his grandmother at the gate. She was ninety-one. She noticed him and asked whether he took the umbrella or not. When she came to know she advised him to take the umbrella. She predicted the possibility of rain in the evening. The gentleman ignored the advice of his grandmother and laughed it away. He answered, 'It is a day full of sunlight. Where from the rain will come'? The old lady kept mum.

In the afternoon suddenly thick cloud appeared and there was a tremendous downpour in the evening. Most of the roads were blocked and the city life was stranded. It was practically impossible for the vehicles to ply on the roads and all the officegoers had to be confined either in their offices or in roads. The gentleman returned at 11.00 p.m. By that time, the old grandmother had slept. There is no equation, which can correlate the prediction of the grandmother and the viability of it. But one conclusion can be drawn. She must have predicted it out of her ocean of experience. Sometimes there are intuitions, which work beyond the capacity of our normal imagination. That's why we must give respect and values to the experience. Two-page science and four experiments are not that much strong to replace the age-old customs and cultures.

68

Sadness Follows Happiness

We should be really thankful to God or the nature, because our thinking process keeps on changing all the time. If the thinking process would have stopped then the whole world would have full of mad people. If the nature had given us the power to click a pause button in our thinking process then certainly all of us would have paused our thinking process. But it doesn't happen. In the natural phenomena there is a combination of happenings. There are series of happenings and some of them are sad and some of them are joyful. In life if the numbers of sad happenings are more then life becomes full of sadness; on the contrary if there is more numbers of joyful incidents then life becomes chequered. But in general, life is a good mixture of both and there are ups and downs in life.

69

You are Ultimately a Six-Feet Space

Often we forget what we are. There is a story about a man who was asked to run in a field to cover a distance as much as he could. There was a condition put by God. God told him, 'You need to run, but before the sunset you must reach the starting point. The distance covered by you will be given to you as a gift.' It was a vast stretch of land. The man was greedy. He ran fast to cover a large area. He kept on running though he felt totally exhausted. Around five in the evening, he found that he covered a considerable distance and he could get huge acres of land provided he could reach the starting point. But the greed was beyond his control. So he wanted to grab few more acres of land and went ahead. After sometime he observed the birds returning to their nest. He guessed that evening was approaching very fast. So he decided to return. He was so tired that it was difficult for him to run. But the condition put by the God was very lucrative. He thought many acres of land could change his fate. Then with a very tired condition he started running towards the starting point. Just before the sunset he reached the starting point. After reaching the point, he started collapsing and within few seconds he fainted and died. After his death he was cremated in the same ground. The funeral pyre was made and it was only six-feet in length. Since he died he was devoid of the land acquired by him. So the conclusion is, 'You may possess huge land, but ultimately you require only six-feet space.'

70

Don't be the Victim of Tension

Tension has become a very common terminology. Another name of tension is stress. In most of the cases we are responsible for this. We created it. Whenever we set very big targets and want to achieve it we get tensed and become unable to reach the target set by us. Depression and tension are the two sides of the same coin.

It would be clear from an example.

In Pune there was a clerk in a government sector. He had only one son. The boy was brilliant. They had a very ordinary life and they used to stay in the government quarters in Pune. The boy had consistent good academic records. He completed engineering degree from a reputed college and after that he joined a good MNC. His father's salary was approximately Rs. 12000 per month, but the boy started with Rs. 35,000 per month along with other facilities. The starting was amazing. For official works he used to go abroad now and then and was also entitled for executive perks. His father gave him only one piece of advice. He suggested, 'My boy, don't change your lifestyle so quickly. Remember that your father is a clerk. Save money. Don't waste it.'

The boy didn't pay any attention to the advice of his old father and started wasting money and after two years he got married. His wife was a software engineer in the same office.

Then after few months, the newly married couple booked a very costly flat in a posh locality and the EMI for the loan taken was approximately Rs. 38,000. Practically his whole salary was the EMI. After a couple of months due to heavy stress of the job, the boy became sick. He was attacked by very severe jaundice. He joined the company before proper recovery and within a few days, the jaundice intensified along with the attack of malaria. Due to very weak condition, the body lost the complete defence mechanism. He was declared unfit by the company and with immediate effect he was terminated. He lost his job. His performance was also found unsatisfactory. Within a week his wife left him. There was the threat of heavy EMI in front of him and his earning was zero. He was also not in a state of good health to join in any other company. He returned to his parents who were abandoned by him after marriage. The flat was taken away from him by the finance company who gave the loan.

This is the colour of life. If anyone wants to lead a life which is beyond his control then stress and tension are obvious. You must use a shoe that fits properly. Otherwise either it will be too tight or too loose. Be careful. False vanity and ego are the main reasons of stress and tension. Explore the inner mind. Don't try to outshine others. These are all vague. The answer is within you. Search it. You will certainly get it. The day you will get the answer you will automatically attain the tranquil state of your mind.

71

Temple Without Deity

Whenever we visit a temple nobody can see God. We see idols and pictures of the deity and many other Gods and Goddesses. The photos and statues of Gods are basically the imagination of human being. All the Gods resemble human beings. Some are in the form of male and some are female. In the kingdom of God, there is no place for the hermaphrodites. Because the kingdom of God is made by the people. Most of the Gods and Goddesses are very good looking. Even an ugly person wants his God to be beautiful, as the most idiot person wants his child to be an intelligent one.

Once a fellow went to a temple and didn't find anything inside the temple. He searched for the images and idols of some God but didn't find anything. Then he came out of the temple and met a very old person. He enquired with the old person about the deity of that temple. The old person was a man of wisdom. He answered, 'This land belonged to my forefathers. There was a God's statue within this temple. It was worshiped for years together by my forefathers. But when I started learning about God then I gradually felt that God is omnipresent. One day I decided not to captivate God within these four walls. When he is omnipresent then he should be free from the bondage of this temple. That very day I immersed the idol of the God in the nearby lake and I saw it melting. I decided not to keep any statue or photographs within this temple. Truly speaking I didn't even want to keep the temple also. For the request of the villagers, I am keeping it and didn't demolish it. I never go inside. Everyday in the morning and evening I feed the stray dogs of this village. There are souls inside them also. Any soul is a part of God. There are millions of people to take care of these so-called Gods and Goddesses but there are few human beings to take care of these street dogs. So I feed them and I consider it as my worship.'

72

Stepping Stone or Stopping Stone

When we start our career, some of us go ahead and some stay stagnant in the same job. For few of us, the first career break becomes the stepping-stone but for many it becomes the stopping-stone. There are various reasons behind any one's stagnancy. Particularly in Government service stagnancy is more; on the other hand in private sector stagnancy is less, growth opportunity is there. The degree of freedom is much more in private sectors. In Government sectors, people remain stagnant because they do not want to take risk. People in Government jobs, don't want to leave it for the security and the pension they'll get after retirement. In old age, financial security matters a lot. In this stage when health doesn't cooperate then pension becomes the only source of earning. But we can't ignore the people serving in the private sector. They too need financial security. In fact, they have more financial security because they can move to better job options. In Government service unless one puts twenty years of continuous service he is not entitled for pension.

I would like to say one thing. The moment you feel stagnant you must try to change the line. Life should not be stagnant. In reality, there is no security. All these securities are pseudo securities. Today if a Government servant is attacked by some dreaded disease like cancer and dies after one year what his family will receive from the Government? If the person is in good post like class-I officer then the spouse will not even get a job. They will get some money left by the person in provident fund and the minimal pension. So one needs to shape his life as long as he is physically capable of doing anything. We often see that very brilliant persons are stagnated, on the contrary many ordinary persons are occupying big posts and positions in different places. Always we can't give the excuse of luck. Luck is there, but it comes at the end in this type of cases. The first and foremost thing is planning with a vision and correct decision. If you have vision you can foresee the future happenings of your life. So don't allow your profession to act as the stopping-stone. Better use your first entry to any profession as a stepping-stone and go ahead and conquer the world.

73

Don't Run After Money

We often say others 'Don't run after money', but we ourselves do that. Running after money is an obsession. There are people in this world who lost everything in life just for money. All of you must be aware of the famous story of king Midas. Money is certainly required, but not at the cost of peace and self-respect. Secondly, by running after money noone can be rich. In this world, the people who are really rich, money runs after them.

I would like to give you a right example from which it will be very much clear that chasing won't produce any effective result. I was in Regional Engineering College, Durgapur, during the year 1982–1986 for my degree, engineering studies in Civil Engineering. I used to stay in the hostel within the campus. The campus was very big and the distance between the main building and hostel was approximately 700 metres. Most of the students used to walk down the distance and some of them used to travel by bicycle. I used to walk through the green bush that encompassed the beautiful campus of my Alma Mater. Presently, it is known as National Institute of Technology (NIT), Durgapur. It is one of the premier technological institutes of Asia.

It would take nine minutes to reach from the hostel to the main building. One day I decided to go fast and I walked very fast and reached the main building. When I watched the time found that I could save only one minute and couple of seconds. I saved approximately 88 seconds (nearly one and a half minute) at the cost of perspiration and increased heart beat. This is the result of chasing. Running or chasing won't produce good results.

Secondly, before running after money you ask yourself why you are running after it. The use of money is an art. You can truly judge the character of a person from his spending habit. People who run after money, are obsessed with materialistic pleasure. There is enough in this world for our need, but to satisfy our greed, the whole world seems to be very less. Whenever we possess anything in excess we start storing it and the moment they are stored, mind starts counting it. So excess wealth blocks our mind. Do you want to be happy? Do you want to be independent like a flying bird? Do you want freedom like a butterfly? If your answer is yes, then you need to run after internal peace, not after money.

As it is not possible to have the cocktail of wine and milk; similarly it's impossible to achieve happiness by running after money. Happiness can be achieved easily provided we change our attitude. With a mind full of greed it's not possible to explore the horizon of happiness.

74

Half Filled or Half Empty

Your perspective to see a problem is a deciding factor in its solution. A sceptic mind always looks at a problem with negative mindset. On the other hand, a positive minded person always looks at a problem with a positive mindset. If you look at a problem with a positive mindset, the problem can be solved easily and the difficulties could be reduced. On the other hand, if one looks at a problem with a negative mindset, the problem becomes more complicated and he faces difficulty in solving it. Mind plays a great role in all the activities of our life. Negative mindset gives birth to preoccupation, and affects the efficiency. If you take a brilliant student and frighten him about a subject and say, 'It is very difficult to clear this subject. It's very hard.' It will certainly influence his mind. He will not be able to perform to his potential. Because now his confidence level has dropped and brain gets blocked by fear and negativity. On the contrary, you take an ordinary student, give him a tough subject and say, 'You can certainly do well. I am well aware of your potential. It's only you who can solve this.' Initially he will be puzzled, but he will not be nervous or demotivated. His moral will be elevated and he will certainly put the best out of him to solve this. So it is always important to look at a problem with a positive mindset. If you look at the number six from the opposite side, it seems to be nine. On the other hand if some one looks at nine from the opposite side, it appears to be six. So it's the question of angle or direction.

So if you fill a glass with water partly then one may say the glass is half-filled, another person can say it is half-empty. The person who thinks it is half empty is a negative minded person and the man who thinks it is half-filled is having a positive mindset. So be positive minded. Don't count what you don't have. Think of the position where you were before five years and where you are at present. The progress may be slow or fast. But there should be a positive and constant growth. Let there be a slow but steady progress. That day will not be very far when your glass will be totally filled.

75

Relation with Your Subordinates

If you want to know about a person then take the feedback from his subordinate. In my life I had never faced any difficulty from my subordinates. On the other hand, my higher authority gave allegation that my subordinates are given indulgence by me. Always I keep one thing in mind. Juniors can't be wrong. There is a famous saying of Napoleon. He said, 'There are no bad soldiers, there are bad officers.' In every office, we see the subordinates are not happy with their boss or the higher authority. There most of the people are hypocrites. They preach one thing and practise other thing. If a subordinate is late by half an hour he is thrashed, but when the boss comes two hours late then some excuse is given. Who will ask him? Pat your subordinate at his shoulder and see the difference.

In my previous office, all the class-III and class-IV staffs used to take the lunch in the corner of the Transportation Engineering Laboratory of the department. In government sector the Class-I officers enjoy a special status. It gives birth to a special kind of ego. Though the meaning of this ego is not clear to me till date. A deputy engineer is a Class-I officer in a government sector. On the other hand, the CEO of a private company is not a Class-I officer. These Class-I officers are empowered to attest certificates, but the moment they are retired the power is ceased. Does it mean after retirement he loses the integrity? It is a very complicated topic to discuss.

One day in my previous office during lunchtime I went to the Class-III and Class-IV people and shared few pieces of breads and curry. The pleasure felt by them is beyond the scope of description. They were happy beyond measure.

The main reason of the hitch is somewhere else. In most of the cases, people consider that their subordinates are their personal servants. Even if you feel that then you must have personal attachment for them. But that is missing. It's just like one-way traffic. While getting the benefit and extracting labour we use our subordinates. But when they need some help then they are not sympathetically handled.

In this regard, I would like to share one of my personal experience. In 1998, I was posted in Government College of Engineering, Karad. During *Deepavali,* I was supposed to come to Pune, because my wife and daughter were in Pune. Among the faculties, I was the second in the seniority in the Civil Engineering Dept. The Principal told he would give permission to only one senior faculty to leave the head quarters. I was already in a mood to come to Pune. I made my mind to see my family members. The senior most professor of the Civil Engineering Department also planned his holiday and he was from Karad. He was a nice person. Seeing my difficulty, he reoriented his programme. He cancelled his visit. He took the leave but didn't leave the head quarters.

Till date I remember the kind courtesy shown by my friend. Still he is a senior professor of Civil Engineering in Govt. College of Engineering, Karad.

Our thinking pattern is very rigid. It requires flexibility. Just think in a reverse way. So please show kind attention to your subordinates. They will never betray you. In 1999, I had a laboratory assistant. He was poor, honest and aggressive. Honest people are generally aggressive. I liked him very much but my HOD didn't like him at all. One day the laboratory assistant came late and that very day I too was late. I reached the institute after him. Before our arrival HOD had a visit to different laboratories. After my arrival, I came to know that the HOD had called me. I met him. He stated, 'Please write in a paper that your laboratory assistant came late. You too came late, but I want to take action only against the lab assistant.' I was surprised. Every boss hates a straightforward subordinate. Straightforwardness is a great quality but in office or service, it could be detrimental. My HOD didn't sustain the straightforward attitude of a mere laboratory assistant. But I declined his instruction. For that I had to give the penalty. After few days the laboratory assistant got the posting near his hometown due to his request, but my confidential report was totally damaged by my HOD. For protecting the subordinate, I had to give the penalty and I accepted it happily. I am happy that I didn't surrender that day and did any harm to a poor fellow for my own benefit.

Now eleven years have been passed. That HOD is retired long back. However, the laboratory assistant still remembers me and whenever he comes to Pune meets me. Our relation is as good as it was in 1999. Nothing is lost, but the bitter deed of an officer is remembered both by my laboratory assistant and me. My laboratory assistant also remembers my sacrifice.

This is life. Respect is not only for the seniors. Juniors should be equally respected. Use it properly in proper place. You will certainly feel better.

76

'E' Means Entry and 'GO' Means Exit i.e. EGO

Ego is the greatest barrier in life. It is a barrier to the progress. Let me share one personal experience, which I knew from my friend. He was a faculty in the Department of Mechanical Engineering in one of the engineering colleges in Pune. He was the DCE (Departmental Controller of Examinations). He used to look after everything related to the examinations of Mechanical Engineering Department. He had direct liaison with the controller of examination of the institute. He used to fix up the dates of the mid-semester examination, collect the question papers from every faculty in sealed condition, allot the seat numbers with the help of laboratory assistant and Class IV employees. His main quantum of work was at the end of each semester. For the oral and practical examinations, he needed to contact the external examiners from other colleges, universities and industries. But for contacting them he didn't have the facility of phone. He was having the facility of intercom only. For the subject concerned HOD was supposed to contact a person from a local industry as an examiner. The HOD knew that gentleman very well. She could have easily contacted that person and requested him to come as an examiner. But for maintaining the so-called protocol, she instructed the concerned DCE to contact the person. My friend said, 'Madam, you are having the facility of phone and you can call him directly. Will you please do that?' The HOD was shocked and angry. She replied. 'How do you expect your HOD to do this silly exam job? Is it the job of HOD? It is the job of the DCE.' Note one point. Being the HOD she feels that exam job is a silly matter. This is EGO. Ego doesn't have a place in the dictionary of people with true wisdom.

Once an IAS officer visited a famous philosopher and in the first meeting he said, 'I am the commissioner of Mumbai.' The philosopher read his body language and pointed his finger to the way to exit. He couldn't tolerate the ego of the commissioner. Whenever a person talks of his post and position he must be egoistic. They must remember that 'E' stands for entry and 'GO' stands for exit. Don't try to boast of the power of your post, and position. Always try to engrave your name in others' heart by love, counselling and tender touch.

77

Illiteracy is not Idiocy

Illiteracy is not idiocy. But often we co-relate these two things. I would like to give an example from which it will be crystal clear. Once in a village, people used to gather in a teashop. The shop owner used to take newspaper. One person used to go through the newspaper everyday. Some people knew that the person was illiterate. One day a person couldn't resist him. He directly commented, 'You are an illiterate. So why you are going through this newspaper?' The person was annoyed and he replied, 'My dear, I am not reading the newspaper, but I am seeing the pictures which are full of information. Even the pictures give me so much knowledge. They are sufficient to enrich my general knowledge.' The person was shocked. From this example, it is clear that illiteracy is not idiocy.

On the contrary literate people can also be idiots. In my teaching life, I came in close contact with many qualified people who are Ph.Ds. Most of them lack common sense. In spite of being doctorates, they lack the common sense. A person without common sense is of no use.

78

Cold Water Bath in a Winter Morning

Many times we lose chances to our timidity. There was a meeting between the director and the faculties in an engineering college. In the meeting, one hundred and forty six faculties were present. On the dais, the director was accompanied by the members of the board of governors. All the faculties were unhappy with the system and they had many grievances. But when the director asked them about their difficulties, no one came forward. The chairman of the board of governors passed the mike to a faculty. He became nervous. But he was the most garrulous person and used to abuse the director and the board of Governors. Nearly ten to fifteen minutes passed but no one spoke even a single word. Though, everybody had the wish to speak. But the question was, 'Who will bell the cat'?

Then nearly after half an hour the director announced, 'It seems to be that all of you are quite happy with the system and you don't have any demand.'

Then suddenly a faculty stood up and said, 'Sir, we have demands. We don't have good seating arrangements; we don't have good computers and internet facility, for taking a print out we need to go to the departmental office. So please do something needful to solve these small problems. Apart from these there are many other problems.' Meanwhile, five other faculties were ready to speak. Then another faculty stood up and said, 'Sir, we don't have good parking facility; we need to take extra lectures for the students who took admission late; but there is no extra payment for that.' Consecutively, twenty three faculties expressed their demands.

The same faculties were keeping mum at the starting for half an hour. It was due to preoccupation. It is just like taking cold water bath in a winter morning. As long as, you don't pour water you are preoccupied. But once you pour water you come out of your conditioning. So the first and foremost thing is to come out of conditioning. So to get rid of conditioning and preoccupation, you need to take decisions quickly. As for example in a cold winter morning, if you don't have access to hot water then you have to take bath in cold water. If it is unavoidable then don't wait. First pour one or two mugs of cold water on your head and get rid of the preoccupation. You will really enjoy the bath, once you get rid of your preoccupation.

79

Discuss but don't Argue

There are many people who derive pleasure in argument. Seldom argument produces any fruitful result. Most of the times both the parties try to dominate each other, and each of them want to prove that he is right. It is always advisable to discuss rather than argue. Most of the times, people are obsessed with some wrong notion, concept or habit. They are not ready to accept their mistakes. On the contrary, they bet and challenge it.

Once in a class of Engineering I was teaching. Suddenly a student stood up and said, 'Sir, you are wrong.' He was a brilliant boy and most of the times brilliancy is coupled with aggressiveness. Other boys felt bad. Because they knew that my concept was correct. The discussion was about moments and bending moments. This topic is beyond the scope of this book. But I was not angry. I accepted the ego of my student. I told him, 'Does not matter. I accept that I am wrong' (knowing that I was correct). But I requested him to go through the textbook at least once.

The next day was Sunday. I used to stay within the campus in the quarters made for the faculties. Nearly at 7.00 a.m. someone pressed the doorbell. Generally the newspaper man used to come late. I opened the door and saw that brilliant boy standing in front of me. He was ashamed of his ego. He came for an apology. But I didn't allow him to do that. On the contrary, I was happy, because he sincerely attended all my classes. In spite of scolding him or allowing him to beg apology, I advised him to reduce his argumentative nature. Because in this world no one likes an argumentative character. There are many great teachers, authors, scientists, players, actors and painters. But if you observe you will find they are popular mainly because of their down-to earth nature. There are many famous cricketers, but why Tendulkar is so popular? It is because of his submissive attitude, down-to-earth and taciturn nature. Never praise yourself. Let others praise you. So don't argue, but have a healthy discussion.

80

Don't Carry Your Office

In cities, people are preoccupied for twenty four hours. Due to the revolution of Internet and computer, we find people working even in their cars while returning from the offices. Even after reaching home they attend innumerable phone calls and most of the people are addicted to internet. Because of their attitude the family members are neglected and they feel irritated. For whom you are working so much? Have you asked this question to your inner being anytime? You have mortgaged your brain for few thousands of dollars to some multinational company. At the cost of salary they have practically purchased your peace and family life. For this I won't make the company responsible. You are mainly responsible for it. In life there must be compartmentalization. If you don't know how to live life in its different aspects and roles you will fail miserably. In this rat race if you stand first then also you will be nothing else than a rat. So it is advisable to have some breathing time.

I saw people discussing about the problems of their office with their family members. Even they discuss it while dining with the family members in front of the little kids. The vicious atmosphere and politics of office reach even their bedroom.

I have a friend. He is a faculty with me in the same department. His wife knows the names of only three faculties of the institute. Even she doesn't know who is the Principal of the college. My friend once commented, 'These professors are not so great that my wife should know them by name.' He is perfectly correct. He separated the family life and office by a strong shield. He never allowed his family members to be unhappy for some of his office matters.

I have seen people carrying the files of their office to their homes. It clearly indicates their inefficiency. No one is entitled to carry out any household activities to his office. Then why one should carry the office files to home? Nowadays people stay in the office for nearly ten hours apart from the travelling time. Over and above, hardly they get four to five hours time to give to their family members.

81

Differentiate Between Doing Things Right and Doing the Right Thing

The name of this chapter seems to be slightly ridiculous. One may ask what is the difference between doing things right and doing the right thing. There is a difference and it requires a hair splitting analysis. There are many disciplined people in this world who do the right things. Even maintaining a regular and disciplined life is also doing things right. But most of them are confined to their daily routine and they do the conventional things and work correctly. But most of them lose interest in life after forty. I saw faculties who are hardly forty, but they started planning their post-retired life. They started taking the reference of their child's success. When asked they said, 'Our life is now over. Now we should concentrate in our child's life.' Here lies the difference. This is not the right thing. The right thing is to be creative at all the ages of your life. Age doesn't become the barrier if your mind is young. If you visit any office in India you will find people with highly depressed, irritated and disturbed conditions. Because most of them have lost interest in life. The moment a person loses interest in life, he becomes saturnine and gloomy. Doing things right is expected of a person. At the same time, one should do right things also. There is no end to doing the right things. As for example writing a good book is a right thing, playing some good game is a right thing, playing some good instrument is a right thing. The more right things you do the more right your life will be. Keep yourself engaged in doing the right things. Certainly your life will be fulfilled with ecstasy and pleasure.

82

Goal Setting

Goal setting is very important in life. Every person must set his goal and one should approach it slowly. Let me give one example. Once we went for an expedition. We were in search of a good hotel and suddenly our vehicle was punctured. I asked a local person about the garage where the car can be repaired. He told the nearest garage is six kilometres away from that place. It was a summer afternoon and I was accompanied by my family members and a few close family friends. There were two ladies and three children. I suggested my friend to wait there in the small roadside hotel and I, myself started for the garage. I immediately set my goal. My goal was to reach there and come back with the mechanic. It was a village road. So there was no chance of getting any sort of vehicle to reach the garage. I started walking. But I never kept in mind that the distance was six kilometres. I thought of walking only one kilometre for six times. The meaning is same, but the difference was that I tried to reach the garage step by step. If you just think that it is a six kilometres distance you would be nervous. In the battle of life win by inches not by miles.

Without a proper goal, life is meaningless, but the goal must not be too big. If any one wants to be a painter it's fine but if anyone wants to get the greatest honour of a painter that is not correct. Whatever you want to be, be that. But don't expect any award out of it. If the performance is good, automatically the awards will follow you. Awards are the outcome of the efforts taken by you in any creative venture. So set a perfect goal and approach it slowly but steadily. To get some regular progress is very important. It is very easy to walk ten kilometres in one day but it is very difficult to walk even half kilometre regularly. So whenever you set a goal, make sure your efforts are consistent and you are respecting the target set by you.

83

Work Smart, Not Hard

I was born and brought up in West Bengal. It's a state in the eastern part of India. In my school days, I found most of my friends mugging up their subjects loudly in the early morning. The parents used to derive a typical satisfaction out of this mugging up of their kids. I never liked this. To be very frank right from my childhood I didn't believe in mugging up a subject. I found my classmates doing the same even in the subjects like Geometry and Algebra. This type of working can be compared with hardwork. Even a bull does lot of hard work in the whole day but what does he achieve out of it? The person who is working as a labour in a Civil engineering site does lot of hard work. But out of this hard work, he can't earn a good livelihood. Due to the lack of education, his total hard work becomes futile. If hard work is coupled with intelligence then only it produces miracle. If a dull boy reads for twelve hours a day, it won't produce any significant result. But if a brilliant candidate reads even six hours per day regularly it will produce miracle. The attitude of the work is very important.

In cricket, a bad batsman may try hard but the ball doesn't reach the boundary. On the other hand, a top class batsman just by a single flick sends the ball to the boundary. It is just the orientation of his wrist, which is nothing but style of batting. The first batsman cites the example of hard work and the second one is the example of smart work. So in life be a smart worker. If smart working style is coupled with hard work then it will produce miracle.

84

Don't Act

It is very unfortunate that with the rapid pace of modernization we have become more and more artificial. We started telling lies for no reason and act even with our very close family members. Even many times the husband and wife act with each other. Acting can be defined as polished lying. Why to lie? I remember in my last birthday, I went to a restaurant with my wife and friends. After a sumptuous lunch, when the bill came I found they had forgotten to add the price of one dish. When I brought it to the notice of my friends most of them advised me to ignore it and pay the amount written in the bill. Very few of them liked my approach. One of them commented, 'Don't be a Gandhi.' I commented, 'I don't want to be Gandhi, but at the same time I don't want to separate myself from my inner being.' One of my friends suggested, 'Pay the bill, if they remember it then just act and say, I didn't check the bill.' For such a small issue I was flooded with suggestions. Why to act for few rupees? Not only few rupees, not even for billons of dollars. Another name of acting is cheating yourself.

Nowadays most of the marriages are like agreements. They are acting. Before the marriage both the partners are engaged and that is the cream period they enjoy. Most of the couple will say the best part of their life is the time between the engagement and marriage. It is a time of no risk. The duo meets for one or two hour regularly. In this particular state both of them are wrapped by the coating of sweet words and good apparels. In this particular juncture there is no struggle. Only there are good promises from both sides.

A man fell in love with a lady. After engagement, they went to a Botanical Garden. The lady wanted a particular variety of flower. It was difficult to access the flower. But to prove his chivalry the person dared to go to the topmost branch and plucked the flower. While coming down he slipped and fell down on a stone. He got a knee injury and severe damage in his genital. After a couple of days, he found there was no erection and after consulting the doctor he learnt that due to the impact of the injury, he has become permanently impotent and no medicine or surgery could cure him. The person was honest to himself. He narrated the matter to that lady. The lady commented, 'You are an idiot. Seeing the intensity of your idiocy it was a prank from my side. I won't marry you. I have decided it long back.'

The person was shocked. One's acting hurt others. Be straightforward. Let you say some bitter words but say it face to face. Initially people may feel unhappy, but once they know your nature they won't be angry with you. Diplomats are good actors. They attack from the back. Beware of them who are having a sugar-coated tongue. No one can be equally sweet natured for twenty-four hours. If it is; then it's acting.

85

Don't Carry Your Raincoat Everyday

Generally in the rainy season, people carry raincoat or umbrella everyday while going to the office. It is also observed that the day you forget to carry the raincoat, that very day it rains. There are people who never forget to carry the raincoat or umbrella. The habit of carrying raincoat or umbrella sometimes become a preoccupation. There are also some people who don't even take out the raincoat or umbrella from their bags. I know people who carry the raincoat till the mid of the autumn for avoiding any kind of risk. But I have a question. If you forget to take your raincoat for one day what will happen? At the most you will be caught in rain and get drenched.

Let me share a very beautiful incident. Long back I was travelling in the city of Kolkata with one of my classmates in a bus. We were supposed to get down at a particular stop. I was conditioned. I started approaching the door through which we had to get down. But my friend suggested me a good thing. He asked me, 'Why you are in hurry? If we fail to get down in the right stop we will get down in the next stop and walk down the distance in the opposite direction.' I was amazed by his suggestion.

The basic thing in life is to get rid of conditioning. Conditioned mind can never go ahead.

86

Don't Check the Talk time After Every Call

Nowadays there is a culture of cell phone. Most of the times, we find people checking the balance after every call. In India, local call rate is one rupee per minute and for STD call, the rate is one rupees fifty paisa to two rupees per minute. But being preoccupied, we check the talk time after every call. Once I asked my house physician, 'Doctor, why don't you use mobile?' She answered, 'I don't want to increase the level of my stress.' I didn't get what she wanted to say. But due to the continuous use of cell phone I too realized that cell phone is a source of stress and irritation. Many times while doing something with intense concentration, I receive calls from some telemarketing executives. It is really irritating and it disturbs your concentration and mood. Resultant of derailed mood is nothing but stress. So cell phone is a source of continuous stress. But in this age of advanced communication, cell phone is becoming a priority for going ahead. What we need is to use the cell phone in a managed way.

87

Deactivating Addiction

Deactivating addiction is a very tough thing. Let us take the example of a smoker. Generally it is very difficult to get rid of any addiction. Often we commit one mistake. Whenever you want to get rid of any sort of addiction then don't leave it overnight. It will create tremendous mental pressure on you. Leave it gradually. Unless we face some disease and forced to leave a bad habit; we continue it. Most of the times due to the forced order of our physicians we are forced to stay away from it. Knowingly we consume it and it can be considered as a slow poison. If the reason is analyzed the conclusion will come out of it. Our need is so much that for time being we try to ignore the ill affects of the addiction. In a recent study it is proved that even if one quits smoking the ill effects of smoking will not be nullified hundred per cent. Secondly, the history of smoking is also considered. The genes undergo a permanent change. Unless we are horrified we generally don't leave the bad habits. Addiction of cigarette is a slow poison. Apart from cigarette there are several other modes of addiction. They are more dangerous too. Any sort of addiction attacks the central nervous system. People argue in a peculiar fashion. To justify the wrong deeds they say; children are becoming the victim of cancer though they are not smoker; on the other hand people with fifty years of smoking history are healthy. Argument doesn't have any end. I too know that smoking can be one of the causative factors for cancer. There is no full proof formula. It is an empiricism. Any empirical formula is derived from repeated observations. There is no full proof mathematical derivation for them. So be careful. As long as you are fit you won't stop arguing, but if any mishap happens then only you will think. Body gives signal well in advance. So reduce it gradually and stop it permanently. Bad habits are enjoyed enough for a long time. Let us try once. Let's have the taste of a disciplined life. Once you are tuned to it, you won't go back to the previous life full of bad habits.

88

There is no Rewind Button in the Keypad of Life

Have you ever felt that with each passing moment you are approaching the ultimate destination? The ultimate destination is nothing else than death. Most of us fight over small issues. Generally we don't bother about our life. We keep on fighting over trivial matters. Until and unless we become sick, we don't realize the values of life.

One of my relatives was attacked by lung cancer. He was with me in Pune. He was admitted in a famous hospital in Pune. One evening I went to see him. When I slowly opened the door of his cabin, I found him looking through the window. The setting sun was clearly visible through the window panes. The whole atmosphere was enveloped by crepuscular darkness. He was lost in thoughts. I didn't want to disturb him. But he guessed my presence. He looked at the door and noticed me standing there. I asked him, 'Are you seeing the beautiful sunset?' He suddenly started weeping and replied, 'My dear, I am not looking at the setting Sun, I am looking at my life. I am also a setting sun. My days are numbered due to dreaded cancer and it is totally spread. I don't know how many sunsets I will be able to see. At the twilight of my life, I realized how small the life is. As if I started my life yesterday.'

I was just listening to him. He wasted his total life in useless gossiping, criticizing others and escaping duties. At the end of his life in deathbed, he realized the importance of life. But unfortunately in the keypad of life there is no rewind button.

In the vehicle of life there is no reverse gear. A stitch in time saves nine. So be careful well in advance. Still there is time. You can't forget the past, you can't delete the past, but certainly you can beautify your present by good deeds, good gesture and positive behaviour. If your present is good, your future is bound to be good. Don't plan much. Just use this moment properly and enjoy this moment. Do the same thing with the forthcoming moments. If you are able to do that then the collective integration will be nothing but enjoying and using your own life. So still there is time. Start it right this moment and go ahead. Always remember that you can't rewind your life even by a single second. So use your time in a proper way.

89

Sun Never Sets

We have a misconception that Sun sets. Actually Sun never sets. When in one hemisphere Sun sets; it arises in another hemisphere.

You must have heard people saying that the garments of a child became short. Actually the garment never becomes short. The child has grown up.

It is the case here. As Sun never sets; your positive minded attitude should also never set. You must be the source of constant energy. It is easy to be a scholar but it is difficult to be a motivator. It is easy to eat alone but it is difficult to share with others. One's attitude must be like a Sun. It is the source of constant energy. The presence of the Sun is taken for granted. The whole world is at the mercy of Sun's rays. But we rarely realize that.

Once I visited a gentleman. He was very humorous. He offered me tea. After the first sip I found there was no sugar in it. After a couple of seconds, he came with a box of sugar cubes. He smiled and said, 'My dear, I intentionally didn't add the sugar, so that you realize the importance of it. So some times I don't pour it intentionally and I want my guest to feel the importance of sugar.'

I was very much impressed by this incident.

Sun never sets. It is present for twenty-four hours. We know even the light of moon is also the reflection of Sun's light only. It is magnanimous. We rarely bother for it. In the same way, we don't bother for them who are at our service. Today, the present generation neglect their health. Health is an irreversible gift of God. The young children neglect the guardians. But the guardians are their well-wishers. The basic human tendency is that we respect them who don't respect us and we disrespect them who care for us. Look at the greatness of Sun and be like it.

90

Love is Truth; Truth is God

People search God in temples, mosques and churches. But God is omnipresent. Once one gentleman was lying in the courtyard of a temple and he felt asleep. After sometime a sentry came and awoke him. He said, 'You are an idiot. Your legs are towards the God within the temple. You must change the direction of your legs. Don't point them towards the God. It is inside the temple.'

The gentleman was least disturbed and annoyed. He answered, 'My dear, God is not confined only to this temple. God is omnipresent.'

Actually most of the people are having wrong conception about the existence of God. Anything good is also God; anything bad is also God. Common people have a staunch belief that whatever good in this world is God. For them a fresh-bloomed flower is God, but a stale dead body is not God. I would like to say a stale dead body is also God. Whatever we see around us is the creation of God. In this world everyone wants to be loved, but there are very few people who want to love others. Have you ever thought in this way? Just do at least once. If you go ahead and love others you will feel a great difference. In this selfish world of sad, bad and mad people please don't follow their footprints.

People are hungry for love and care. You try to be slightly different. Just love people and automatically you will very easily reach the heart of the people. The heart of people means heart of God. When a famous astronaut returned from space he was asked whether he could meet God in the space. Because common people always point their fingers towards the sky while talking of God. That famous astronaut couldn't reply. But a famous philosopher explained it very beautifully. He explained, 'For exploring the God, don't dig your outer world, you need to dig your inner being.' There is no truth in this world bigger than love. Love is eternal and it is the biggest force of the world. It is even stronger than the total nuclear power of the world. Proper love can counsel even a criminal. The tender touch of love has unimaginable power.

Once in a jail there was a criminal. He was very aggressive and adamant. The police used to abuse him and torture him. He was also very stubborn. There used to be regular fight among them. Once one young IPS officer was posted in that jail as the in-charge. He came to know about this and noticed everything. First, he scrupulously went through the past records of the criminal and tried his best to have some idea about the psychology of that criminal. One day the officer went to his cell and presented him a guava. The inmate was crestfallen. In his whole tenure of jail nobody talked to him with respect. He was amazed. He was touched at core and started crying. He tried to touch the feet of the officer, but couldn't. Because he was behind the bar. The inmate was qualified. Then by gradual counselling the officer totally transformed that criminal to a normal human being. Every inmates and police in the jail noticed the metamorphosis in the behaviour of the criminal. It was amazing. Whatever change took place is due to the sheer love of that police officer. Love can transform everything. We need not spend anything for loving others. But still we don't go for it. Generally we are all cynics and sceptics. We try to pull the legs of our colleagues. We criticize our colleagues at their back. Always we go for bargaining. We forget that life is a gift. We completely misuse our life. From the dictionary of common people the word 'help' is gradually being erased. Just help others, love others and wish the good of others. There is no bigger truth than love and through this truth you can reach threshold of God's kingdom. Truth is the only bridge, which takes you to the domain of God. Truth joins the two extreme things. They are Love and God. In fact they are not different. Love is the manifestation of God's will within any soul. God is the ultimate truth. God can be compared with an abstract thing which is composed of love only. It's only love; which is the prerequisite for an eternal quest for peace.